CHRONICLE OF A LAST SUMMER

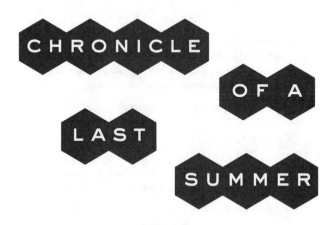

A NOVEL OF EGYPT

YASMINE EL RASHIDI

UNCORRECTED PROOF

TIM
DUGGAN
BOOKS

NEW YORK

Copyright © 2016 by Yasmine El Rashidi

All rights reserved.
Published in the United States by Tim Duggan Books,
an imprint of the Crown Publishing Group, a division of Random House LLC, a Penguin Random House Company, New York.
crownpublishing.com

CROWN and the Crown colophon are registered trademarks of Random House LLC.

Library of Congress Cataloging-in-Publication Data
<~?~CIP data>

ISBN 9780770437299
eBook ISBN 9780770437305

PRINTED IN THE UNITED STATES OF AMERICA

Jacket design by
Jacket photograph by

1   3   5   7   9   10   8   6   4   2

First Edition

Dedication TK

PART ONE

SUMMER 1984, CAIRO

THE HOUSE WAS BLISTERING. Mama had drawn in and closed the wooden shutters hours earlier. Damp towels lay rolled on windowsills. The heat still seeped in. She now sat at one corner of the sofa, gray phone receiver in one hand pressed to her ear, plant mister in the other. She sprayed her face at intervals. Mama had always said the heat never bothered her. It was how she was made. That summer had been different. I sat at her feet staring at the muted TV screen, getting up and flipping between channels. Channel One. Channel Two. The third channel stopped its broadcast at one p.m. There were only two programs for children. I flipped hoping I might find something. In the corner of the room was Granny's old metal fan. It clicked and whirred, drowning out Mama's English-laced Arabic. I could make out none of the conversation, except to take note when she switched to French. It was the single language she spoke that I still didn't know. She seemed to use it more often that summer.

I had no way of measuring time, but we sat like that for hours. Ossi appeared now and then at the doorway and meowed. Mama ignored him. He was gray with long hair. Mama had said it was a bad idea to have a Persian. If one were to have a cat, it ought to be a local, a *baladi*. Baba said let the girl have what she wants. He brought him home in the palm of his hand one day. The day I turned five. I wanted to call him Fluffy. Mama said Fluffy was not a proper name. She called him Osama. Baba never touched him again. He was allergic, even though his hands were huge. He would put me onto his palm and lift me into the air. I would sit perched like that as he watched TV. I missed Baba's hands, especially his giant fingers. He would make a hook out of them and pretend he was hooking my neck like a fish, pulling me close to kiss him. I loved the way Baba smelled. You could smell him everywhere in the house, especially on the sofa. Even when he went on trips his smell would still be there. It had gone away this time. I was waiting for him to come back. Every day after school I would get out my class notebook and turn back the pages to the one with the green star in the corner for the day he left. I would flip to the next page. Then the next page. I counted until I reached fourteen. I kept counting until the page we used in school that day. Fifty-seven. I couldn't tell how many extra days it had been.

It was July, but I was still in school. My cousins had four months of summer holiday. Sometimes five. We only had one. It was the English school. In Arabic school there was no homework. The teachers didn't make enough money to correct it. I wanted to be in Arabic school like my cousins. It wasn't fair. Mama shook her head. Four months of summer would make of me a listless child. Too much holiday was bad for character, Mama said. Poor posture was also a sign of it. That summer it had become a concern. Mama finished her phone call and told me to walk across the room with a book on my head. She made me do this each afternoon. I made it like a game. I especially liked when the book began to slip. It tilted to the right, and I felt it. I bent my knees. It was as if I were going to jump, take off, but I slid back up, pushing my right shoulder. It slipped back into place. It only ever slid to the right. The next time it fell. It was an old book with a thick blue cover. It said SUEZ. It hit the parquet floor with a thud. I glanced back at Mama nervously. I saw she wasn't watching.

It was a school night, but Mama had stopped paying attention to time. I stayed up late with her. I took out my sketchbook. I drew. Fish. The bottom of the sea. Myself swimming with them too. The teacher shook her head. She told me I had to watch myself, I was a dreamer. I turned to the TV. They were replaying pictures of starving children in Ethiopia. Every day we watched them. Mama had a friend from Ethiopia. She taught me how to count to ten in their language. Whenever she came for lunch she said a prayer before she ate. She said it was for the famine. She told me to look at the food on my plate and remember how lucky I was. With each bite I should remember Ethiopia. Maybe I should send my lunch to Ethiopia? Every time I see the starving children on TV, I say a prayer. I don't know what to say, but I put my head down like Kebbe and move my lips. I then say *Allahu Akbar*, like Grandmama does. I whisper so that Mama can't hear. There are also starving children in Cairo, but they never show them on TV. I see them in the streets on the way to school. They sell lemons at the traffic light. Three of them sleep in a cardboard box under the bridge next to our house. One of them has hair like mine. I know if I stand next to her, the top of our heads will meet. I want to talk to her, but when I smile and start to roll down the window one day, Mama tells me to look away. I'm not to encourage such behavior. I turn my head down. I look at her from the corner of one eye.

After the famine they replay the documentary about Sadat. They show him with his wife and children. They show him meeting important people. They show him at the parade where he was killed. I was three and three-quarters when they killed him. It was the day of Mama's birthday. We were watching TV. Mama put her hands to her mouth. Baba stood up. They gasped, then were silent, then Mama started saying Quran. I was too young to remember. Baba told me everything about Sadat. He did very good things and very bad things. Making peace with Israel was very bad, Baba said. He didn't like the Israelis. They were buggers. Mama grumbled that he shouldn't use the word again. They wouldn't tell me what buggers were, but I knew they were bad. Everyone we knew hated the Israelis, except for one of Baba's cousins. Baba raised his eyebrows at him and shook his head. He turned and looked into my eyes. He had signed his name to fight in the war. It was important to be loyal to my country.

Next they play the video of the new president,

Mubarak. He was sitting next to Sadat when he was killed. They said it was a miracle he wasn't killed too. It was something from God so they made him president the next week. Now he was always opening a new factory. They show him cutting the ribbon and shaking people's hands. Baba said it was the making of a pharaoh. I got up and changed channels. Channel Two. The black and white film with Ismail Yaseen. It screened on Thursdays after school. They would play things in order and many times over. The TV was mostly boring but Mama only let me watch videotapes on weekends. She said only boring people got bored. I felt bored every day after school. I got up and put the last tape into the VCR. I hit rewind. It made a sound like an airplane passing. Mama tutted. When it finished rewinding it clicked three times. I pressed eject. It made a rumbling noise, then squeaked as it came out. I put it back in its case and onto the shelf next to the five VHS tapes Baba said were for me. There were other tapes on the higher shelf. They were adult. I went back to Mama's feet. She was on the phone changing languages between English and Arabic and French. I heard her say it was the only thing she had. I knew she was talking about the house. *They can forget it*. She switched to French and I heard her say Baba's name.

I bring out my writing notebook from school. We have to write a story from our day. I draw a blue frame around the page. In one corner I write the date. I count down four lines and write: *I am sitting with Mama waiting for the power to cut.* At the bottom I draw a picture of Mama on the sofa. I draw a vase with sunflowers like in the films. I watch the flickering TV screen until the power cuts. We don't say anything when it happens. It cuts every evening, then there is silence. Even from the street all sound stops. We stay in the living room, not moving, until it comes on again. Some days Mama gets up and moves to the balcony. She takes the phone. The cord is so long it also reaches the bathroom. Usually she just stays on the sofa misting herself. The cuts last one hour. Sometimes two. Some days, in the winter, they skip a day. We all have power cuts. Only three of my friends at school don't have power cuts. Their fathers are important. One of my best friends has a grandfather who is important. He is dead now, but they are still important. They never have power cuts. Mama also says the Sadats never have them. They are related to us, but not close enough for our power cuts to stop too.

The lights come on again. The TV flickers, then screams with sound. Mama sighs and shakes her head. I press mute. She gets up and comes back with a tray. I have the same dinner every night. Every night Mama tells me to chew slowly. I count. Twenty, twenty-one, twenty-two. Sometimes I reach thirty. Baba didn't mind how I ate. He liked food more than Mama. Once, after Baba left, Aunty came to the house and told Mama she had to make an effort with her food. That day Mama was crying. I gave her a tissue and stood next to her. She patted my head. She didn't seem to make an effort after that. Mama was thin. Nobody else we knew was thin like Mama. Except on TV, but only in American films. I take a bite of my grilled cheese sandwich.

After a while *Dallas* comes on Channel Two. It runs six nights a week, and everyone watches. I go to the kitchen balcony and watch people watching in the building next door. Everything is dark except the screens. I imagine myself in the flat with the three sisters. I wish I had sisters. I go inside. Mama asks me to turn up the volume. Her dinner tray is on her lap. I watch Mama chew. She chews slowly, like Nesma did.Mama said that Nesma dying was like losing a child.She was my aunt, but they said she was like my sister. She had Down syndrome. It was also about hormones, but not Baba's kind. That kind was only for men, to make them big. People told Mama they admired her. One lady said that anyone else would have hidden Nesma away. I imagined her in a cupboard. How would she eat? Some days after school I would sit in my cupboard imagining I was hidden away. I waited for them to find me. Baba did, but after he left nobody took notice. Mama did everything for Nesma. I heard her crying on the phone once because someone had made fun of Nesma at a restaurant. She said people think Nesma doesn't understand. I knew she understood. I wished I had known last summer would be our last holiday together. I came home from school one day, and at the gate I heard my name. I looked up. It was Nana, Mama's friend, in the building across the street. She was on her balcony, waving. *Come.* Her building had an old glass elevator that rattled as it went up. You could see all the wires. They were black and greasy. I took the steps. I never remembered what floor they were on, but Abu Ali their neighbor had Quran written on his door. Mama and Nana said this was terrible. Sometimes when I saw Abu Ali he would tell me *Al Salam Alaykum.* Mama told me I should never respond. Only nod your head. Since when do we say *Al Salam Alaykum.* If you answer, say *Sabah El Kheir.* Grandmama was always reading Quran and saying *Al Salam Alaykum.* I told Mama. She said I was too young to understand. I reached Nana's floor. The door was open. She told me to come inside, then hugged me. Nana never hugged. Bad news. Nesma died and I would be staying the night. I screamed. I screamed so hard my voice stopped, like in the dream. I wanted to go home. She made me sit at the dining table and put a plate with rice and okra and *escalope panée* in front of me. She told me I had cried enough. Mama didn't let me eat *escalope panée*. I ate it quickly. I fell asleep that afternoon and woke up again after eighteen hours. Nana said she had never seen anyone sleep so long.

When Nana let me go home, there were many people in the house dressed in black. Mama had on a white scarf. A man was sitting cross-legged on Granny's armchair reciting Quran. Mama never let anyone put feet on the furniture. Our house was Granny's house. Mama was born in it. It was two floors and like a castle. The garden was filled with trees. We had mangoes, figs, tangerines, sweet lemons. There was also a tree that grew from the seeds Mama threw out of the window when she was a little girl. Custard apple. We even had a coffee tree that Mama's friend brought us from Ethiopia. Under it was a wishing spot. Any wish you made would come true. Baba had built me a playhouse in the corner. It was wooden and painted red. The Nile was across the street. We could see it from the upstairs balcony. Mama said our house was plain but unique. Baba called it modern. People would take pictures. There were little windows at the top, near the roof, tiny, in threes, like secret rooms. There was a round window on one side, and a triangular window on the other. There was a secret box of treasures that Granny hid in the staircase when the house was being built. Granny lived downstairs with Nesma, and I would come home from school and find their floor full. People I knew. People I didn't know. We would have lunch in Granny's dining room, and Mama and Baba would come down too. Granny would sit at the end of the long table. She would ring her silver bell and Abdou would come in from the kitchen. Abdou was dark and from Sudan. He would go on holiday every summer and bring us back peanuts. Sometimes I would sit in the kitchen as he cooked. Abdou was always making *maashi*. He lined green peppers and zucchini on the counter and went through them, one by one. He held each vegetable like a tennis ball and with a knife made a circle on the top. With his special sharp-edged spoon he would scoop, bringing out the insides. *It's all in the wrist.* He taught me. Making dessert was the best. We picked mangoes from the garden that Abdou cut into pieces and put in the freezer. I licked the skins that were left. Abdou would tell me stories about

Sudan. Once Egypt and Sudan were like one country. It was because of the English. They made some countries theirs. They divided other countries. Abdou didn't like the English or the Americans. He told me they were trouble. If there weren't any English or Americans the world would be a different place. He said they should mind their own business. When I asked Mama, she said I had to be careful what I said about the English and the Americans. Mama said that Abdou was the one who should mind his own business.

After Granny died, Abdou left. Mama closed downstairs and Nesma moved upstairs with us. Everyone stopped coming for lunch. I missed Abdou, but sometimes he came to visit. I would look out of the window after school and see him coming down the street. I would run down and wait for him in the garden. He brought me things. Once he had a bag of *'asalia*. It was like sugar but yellow and healthy. Another time he had roasted watermelon seeds. He even bought me long stalks of sugarcane from the cart that passed through the streets. We ate them in the garden. I waited to see what he would bring next. Then one day he stopped coming. I waited day after day at the window but never saw him again. No one went downstairs anymore. Mama said it depressed her. It was dark and smelled of Granny. I remember Granny's smell. Mama said her smell was musky amber. It was an ancient smell. She said Granny's smell and spirit were trapped downstairs. This meant ghosts. Or maybe the devil who was also a ghost. Mama was always talking about the devil. They also told us about the devil on TV. If we were naughty, the devil would become one with us. I was terrified of the devil and became scared of downstairs. When Nana took me home, we went in from the back door of the house. That was the door to Granny's floor. I hadn't been downstairs since she died. Mama was waiting for me. She told me to kiss everyone and go upstairs to my room. When the people left, I could come out again. It wasn't healthy for a little girl to be around so much black. I stayed there for three days. Ever since that day, whenever I come home from school, I am frightened to look up. I don't want to find Nana on her balcony. I am also scared to look at people in black because it might make me sick, but then I peek.

Mama stopped talking about Nesma, but once on the phone I heard her say that she had a dream about her and woke up in tears. After a while she also stopped talking about Baba.

· · ·

Mama never woke up early. I dressed myself. My uniform was on my chair. Mama put it out at night. The socks she left out were odd. One was shorter than the other. I folded the long one inside itself to make it look the same. I went to the kitchen to make my sandwich. I opened the fridge and looked inside. The English girls at school all had apples for lunch. Green ones. Red ones. They bought them from the embassy. We only had apples when we went to Port Said, and they only had red ones. Baba used to drive us some Saturdays. He would buy shaving cream and razors. Mama would buy bars of soap in colored wrappers. The soap from Port Said was better. In Cairo it was big brown blocks cut with a knife. They sold it on the pavement. You had to wash the soap before you used it. I liked the bars from Port Said. They were smooth and pink. They smelled of perfume. They also sold chocolates in Port Said, but Mama said they were too expensive. The only chocolate we had in Cairo was filled with caramel that stuck to your teeth. I couldn't have it because Mama said it was inappropriate for a young girl to be pulling at chocolate. We ate chocolate only when Baba came from a trip and brought back Toblerone. I got a triangle every Friday. We had been to Port Said the week before Baba left. The apples we bought were finished. Mama had cut them into eighths. She squeezed lemon over them so they wouldn't turn brown and gave me an eighth after lunch every other day. Sometimes I asked for more, but I couldn't have any because I had to learn restraint. When I asked Mama if we could go back to Port Said when Baba returned, she told me she was busy right now. I also asked if we would go to the beach when Baba came back. She said it would be a long summer and looked away.

In the car once Baba explained that it was because of Sadat we had apples and nice soap. It was like Christmas every day after the deprivations of Nasser. Nobody could have anything then. Mama replied that it was better not to have too much from the outside. It created greed. They argued. I looked out of the window and tried not to hear them. There was nothing to look at but I imagined there was a battle in the desert like in the film they always played on TV. I take out the soft white cheese and a loaf of *fino* bread. Mama sends Mustafa the *bawab* to buy it on Saturday mornings. She gives him twenty-five piastres, and he comes back with thirteen loaves. Mama mutters how he takes two for himself. She then empties the loaves from one bag to another. The bakery bag is black. They use black bags to hide the dirt. I sit at the kitchen table eating my cornfleks watching her. I mix the cornfleks in the milk until they become soft. My favorite part is the milk at the end, after the cereal is gone. I want to ask why Mustafa takes the bread. Why doesn't she tell him off? I want to ask many things but Mama doesn't like me asking too many questions. I spread a piece of white cheese in my bread and put the box back in the fridge. I wrap my sandwich in newspaper. I wish I had an apple.

I am late. The school bell has already rung. I tiptoe into the hall for assembly and stand at the back. The headmaster will tell me later not to be *tardy* again. He puts a mark in the book by my name. Four marks then a diagonal one through it, like hangman. There are three of these now. The first time they asked I said the driver was late. Then I said the car stopped. Then my stomach hurt. Then I stood and looked at the teacher and turned my head down to my shoes. He growled through his moustache, *The timing of the locals.* This time the headmaster asks about Baba. He is still away. He doesn't say anything for a long time, then pats my shoulder and asks me to set my alarm clock for earlier. I tell Mama when I get home. I had become *tardier* that summer. My alarm clock rang and I would get out of bed and get dressed. We had to tuck our shirts in. Girls couldn't wear trousers. We had to wear our hair in ponytails. No jewelry. I started to spend longer looking in the mirror. Everyone said I looked like Baba. I started to go into Baba's study. The door was kept closed but Umm Ahmed would go in once a week to dust. On those days I would come home from school and find Mama at Baba's desk. She would be sitting, looking at nothing. I would go to my room. In the mornings I started to go and sit at the desk too. Baba had a big leather chair that swirled. It was my favorite chair in the house. I could almost see the top of the desk from it. There were piles of papers. Nothing I could understand. Most them were in Arabic. Numbers. Some papers had the American flag. Others had the Russian flag. We learned world flags at school. Some of the papers also had the old Egyptian flag. It was green with stars and the moon. We never learned this in school, but Granny had told me.

Baba's office was the only place that still smelled of him, but only a little and only if you opened the drawers. I would open the third drawer of his desk and put my nose to it. I opened it just a crack so that the smell wouldn't escape. There was a picture of Grandpapa on the desk. It was black and white, but his lips were painted pink. Grandpapa looked like a walrus. He was fat. Mama said businessmen liked to be fat. It was a sign of prosperity. On the wall behind the chair were pictures of Baba shaking people's hands. I knew

I was going to be late for school because I could hear the driver honking the horn of our small white car. It was an old car and the leather of the roof was falling in. The driver took a stick from the garden and put it across the roof on the inside to hold it up. He honked five times five minutes before we had to leave. For every minute I was late he would honk twice. Nobody told him to honk like this. Mama asked him to stop. He kept honking. He honked as we drove, even on empty streets. Baba said it was a product of circumstance. People like to be heard, and this was the only way to assert oneself in a country like this. Mama and Baba said *it* was the worst thing a person could become. I started to wait longer, sitting in Baba's chair.

We took the same route to school each day. Down our street past the Libyan embassy then right. The building on the corner was where the important journalist Hassanein Heikal lived. When Baba read the newspaper in the morning he would nod and say that Heikal knew. I didn't know what he knew, but Baba pointed to his building each time we drove by. I wondered if he had power cuts. Baba also said once that a famous American writer used to live there too. Her name was Maya. She was black and friends with Malcolm X. She worked at a newspaper downtown. Baba said Maya was an angel. I told the American girl at school about Maya being an American angel and living on our street. She laughed and said Angelou then skipped away. I watched. Her yellow plait bounced on her back.

My favorite part of the drive was the long street on the Nile. There were people rowing boats in the mornings. You could see them through the fence along the river. When Mama was little there were no fences. She would take her book and beach chair and walk down to the water. She would sit reading with her toes dipped in. The Nile was blue. Then it became green. Mama would never dip her toes in the water now, but Grandmama said that to have a sip of the Nile is like drinking ancient magic. If you make a wish it comes true. She said the same about the white beads around her neck. When I see her I put my fingers on them and make wishes in my head.

We drive around the island to school. I make a map in my head each Monday. Cars, signs, shops, pieces of garbage, donkeys, billboards, food carts, posters stuck to lampposts, villas. I memorize them and give them numbers, like points. If they are still there the next day I get the points. On Fridays I add them up and write them on a small paper that I keep in my shoe. There are some things that are never there the next day. There are some things that are always there. Like the billboard with the president on it. There are some things that are there for a very long time, then disappear. One day they pulled down the white villa on the Nile. Mama said they did it overnight so that nobody would know. The red car that was parked on the corner by our house piled with dust was also always there. It was always on my map, for ten points. It got dirtier and dirtier. One day someone pushed their finger into the dirt and wrote a bad word on the glass. The car was still there, but with the word I didn't get the points. Then one day the police came and took it away. I didn't see, but I heard Mama on the phone. The police would come sometimes and take things. They took the cart of the peanut seller on our street. They took the kiosk by the school that sold chocolates and Cleopatra cigarettes by the one. They took the man who worked for Uncle Mohsen. They also took the boy who cleaned cars at the garage next door. In the cartoon *Abla Fatiha* they told us that if we were naughty, they would take us too. I heard a teacher say that they took my friend's papa. When I asked Mama she *tssssked* and told me it was nonsense. Uncle was in Geneva. I wondered if that was where Baba was too.

Once we had a new cleaning lady who stole from Mama. She never came back, but the police caught her. Mama and Baba took me with them to the prison to see her. They wanted to make sure she was the right thief. We went in Baba's car, over the bridge, past buildings, until we were far, where the desert was. They took us inside. We went up dirty stairs. It was dark and smelled of pee. She was in a small room behind bars like a cage. There was a wooden stool like Abdou used to have and a dirty red towel hung from the wall. When she saw Mama she started crying and saying sorry. *Sorry. She was sorry.* The policeman shouted to her *shut up.* He used the bad word. She kept crying, *sorry.* Mama turned her face away and took my hand. She squeezed it and pulled me. I didn't know if she had accepted her sorry. I wanted to ask but my lips were sealed. The prison was frightening. People were screaming and shouting from places I couldn't see. One man looked at us from behind bars and roared like a lion. His hands were black. We went down and waited for Baba in the car. Later I heard Baba say that they had gone to her house in the night and taken her away. They made a racket so that everyone in the neighborhood could hear. They took her away in front of her children. What would they do with her? He didn't answer. Every time I see a policeman going into a building I think maybe they will take someone away. In class I write a story called "The Disappearing People." I write about going to the prison. I write about the people they take away. It happens only at night. My teacher gives me zero out of ten and says I shouldn't be writing such things at my age. At home I cry to Mama and show her the story. She reads it and sits without saying a word on my bed. I think she is angry. It scares me when Mama is angry. Sometimes she shouts when she is angry and sometimes she is just quiet. The quiet angry is much worse.

The teacher writes a date on the blackboard. The Independence of Great Britain. We don't have to remember it this term, we will come back to it later. A boy in the front puts his hand up. He is from India. Nanchal is the only one who asks questions. He asks about the Independence of Egypt. The teacher tells him we will be concentrating on British history for now. Nanchal tells her that he has already learned these things in India. It is his first year at school with us. He thought that in Egypt he would learn new things. He is *eager* to learn about Egypt and its great civilization, *eager* to learn about when Egypt stopped being a colony. I have never heard the word *eager* before. The teacher tells him to see her after class.

At break I go to the bars shaped like an igloo. The

boy from primary five with a ponytail is hanging upside down. I tell him Baba is away on business. He
doesn't care. I watch him. He pushes his waist into
the air and swings. His arms fly and move in circles.
Again. He twists and jumps into the air. He lands
next to me. I notice his shoes. They are not proper
shoes, and he has fluorescent laces. *They call me Chief,*
he says. His hands are on his hips. I look at him and
don't know what to say. He tells me he saw God earlier. He was wearing white and blue stripes and had
on spectacles. He was writing in a big book like the
headmaster's one. What was he writing? The secrets
of life. He asks me where Baba is. I think maybe he
is in Geneva. I ask him if God can see everything.
Does God know where everyone is and what they are
doing? God was very busy today. How does he know
God is writing the secrets of life if he doesn't know
Arabic? God was not writing in Arabic. The language
of the book is English. Our teachers tell us this too.
Every morning they read from the Bible and talk
about God. I tell Chief about the writing on Abu Ali's
door. It's the words of God and it's Arabic. Mama says
it's bad. His dad says the same thing. His dad works
at the American embassy. I tell him that Uncle says
the people at the American embassy are spies. Baba
too. He knows lots of spies. Once after a trip I heard

him tell Mama about meeting a famous Egyptian spy. But the Egyptian spies are not bad like the American ones. Uncle and Baba said the American spies at the embassy are trouble. The only embassy we go to is the English one, and I don't think they are spies. They take us there for school on the queen's birthday. We have to dress smart and sing to God so that he saves the queen. Otherwise she might die. Mama makes me wear shiny shoes and a red dress with frills. I ask her not to make me wear shiny shoes. *Please not the dress with frills.* The other girls wear what they want. She doesn't care what other people do. We are not other people. We are not English. I know she wouldn't like it if I had a boy friend with a ponytail. If Baba were here he wouldn't mind. He would tell Mama to relax and that a little bit of mischief built character. When Baba was a boy, he used to take books from the library and hide them under his shirt. He also used to write things on his arm in tiny writing before tests. Grandmama told me. Baba laughed when I asked if it was true. I tell Chief about going to the desert with Baba. He has a big tile factory in the desert and we ride his Jeep fast up and down the dunes. Maybe he could come with us to the desert when Baba came back? Baba would like him. He says it would be awesome and asks when he's coming back. My shoulders drop. I stare at him. I don't know. He's late. He shrugs. It will be awesome. I repeat the word *awesome* to myself as we go back up to class. When I say awesome in front of Mama later she tells me to mind my language.

The teacher tells us to curve our letters. *Relax your hand.* She looks over our shoulders. She slaps a wooden ruler on her palm. Taps the wall. Doorknob. Dictionary. Desk. Another desk. My desk. My handwriting is too small. *It won't do.* She gives me another sheet. *Make your letters bigger.* She tears one boy's paper. He is a disgrace. *Go and wash your hands.* We laugh. She claps her hands. *Silence.* The girl in the front giggles. Her father is the Ambassador of England. The teacher never tells her off. Mama says my handwriting is like Baba's. I try to make it bigger. We hand in our sheets. For the rest of the class, we will be writing a letter. We can write it to anyone we know. On the blackboard she writes: Mother, Father, Sister, Brother, Grandmother, Grandfather, Uncle, Aunt, Teacher, Friend. I wonder if I should write a letter to Mama. Mama is always writing letters. Sometimes when she is having her siesta I go through the drawers of the bookshelf and find letters. Some of them are to Baba. I don't know if they are letters she gave Baba or not. One of them is about money. I don't know if they are new letters or old letters. I showed Dido a letter once and he shook his head hard and said Mama was upset. It explained a lot, but maybe I was too young for these things. Dido's real name is Dawood, but everyone calls him Dido. He is the oldest cousin and says my school will repress me. It is the only thing left of the monarchy and colonialism. Mama and Baba are antirevolutionary for sending me there. *Where did their nationalism go?* He also says the Palestinians are our brothers. I need to remember these things even if I don't understand them yet. When I'm older I will thank him. He pats my head. Dido is my favorite cousin. Maybe I should write my letter to him. I look at the lines of my notebook for a long time. Everyone else is already writing.

I will write to Nesma. I will tell her about Mama's letter to Baba. I will tell her about Baba in Geneva and the house being empty now. I will tell her that Mama washed and ironed all her clothes and they are still in her cupboard. I might tell her that I stole Mama's upset letter to Baba and hid it under my mattress. I will also tell her that we found a spell under my mattress. It was on a small paper folded many times filled with tiny writing. When I showed it to Mama she whispered to herself, then got a woman to the house who walked around me with incense saying

Quran. She burned the spell on the stove and pricked it with pins. Mama threw the ashes from the window and said Quran. Sometimes Mama says Quran is okay and sometimes it's bad. This time it was to remove the devil from me. I cried. Mama said there was nothing to be afraid of. It was just something that happened sometimes.

Dido is outside the gate after school. He is wearing a black T-shirt with splashes of blood. Colored string bracelets fill his wrist, the kind Mama calls scruffy. He came back from the beach for a football match. Everyone says he will be famous. I hug his waist and he kisses my head. He says we can go to the shop before we go home. All the older children from school go to the shop. They used to go to the kiosk to buy a cigarette until the police took it away. Now they go to the shop. The shop isn't really a shop. It's a hole in a wall with a wooden counter and shelves in the back. Only one person fits in it. When it's closed it looks like a garage. The shop isn't allowed to sell cigarettes by the one but they do. You have to buy something else too if you want a cigarette. Most of the boys and girls buy Chipsy or a can of juice. The man uses black bags like the kind the bread comes in. Dido asks me what I want. An ice cream cone. I have to get something else. A red packet of Chipsy. He tells the man to *add two to it*. The man tells him the price. Dido tells him to do him a favor. *Impossible*. Come on, be a man. They talk more. Dido puts the money in the man's hand and slaps his shoulder. He owes him. I want to sit on the brick and eat my ice cream. Dido stands over me. I see him take two cigarettes from the bag and put them in his back pocket. I watch the English girl whose father is ambassador choose four packets of chips and two juices. She gives the man one pound. Her money is always new. He puts it in the drawer and looks past her. She stares at him. Another boy comes from behind. The man nods at him. *A chocolate*. He gives him the coins. He sits on the pavement near me and unwraps it. It's the inappropriate kind. The English girl is still there. The man turns his back to her. I watch. She waits longer. After a while she walks away. Once I gave the man ten piastres for a sweet that cost five. I put the money in his hand. He didn't say anything. Someone came after me and asked for a Chipsy. I waited like the English girl, then walked back to find the driver.

Dido and I walk home. Mama took the driver on an errand and will be back later. When? Later. But we can do anything I want until then. He asks about my day. *The teacher caught me saying a word in Arabic and made me do lines. I had to write a hundred times, I will not speak Arabic.* He shakes his head. *The teacher is mean because she has never been married. Grandmama says that only when a woman is married is she fulfilled.* He shakes his head more. I ask him to tell me a story. He holds my hand. We turn the corner onto the long street that goes from one side of the island to the other. Dido tells me it was named after the revolution. Have I learned about the Free Officers? I shake my head. *They launched the revolution that saved Egypt from the British. They got rid of the king. They made Egypt independent. Baba's uncle was a Free Officer. He was the most principled man in the revolution. He resigned as vice president when the revolution goals were forgotten. He went and hid at Grandpapa's house. He put his diaries under the mattress. He stayed there for five days. When they came looking for him, they found him watching TV. Baba was on his lap.* Then what happened? He shrugs. *But the children of the men who made the revolution are corrupt,* he says. I look at him. To be corrupt means to steal. My friend's grandfather was the president and great, but his children . . .

We walk past the key shop. The key man came to our house three times after Baba left when Mama forgot her keychain inside. He put a flat piece of metal like a knife in the side of the door and opened it. Mama thanked him and asked God to protect him. Afterwards she said she didn't trust him. He made her uncomfortable. It was too easy to steal a house. She would start locking the door from the inside at night.

There are piles of newspapers on the pavement outside the juice shop. Dido takes one and puts a coin in the man's hand. He wants to read the interview with the supreme guide who is the ruler of the Muslim Brotherhood. The president banned them from running in elections for parliament and now there is a long interview about it. The journalist who conducted it is courageous, or he might be a Brotherhood member too. How does he know if someone is Muslim Brotherhood? He squeezes my hand. *It's complicated.* I hold his hand tighter. We are quiet, then Dido tells me the elections were two months ago. Why did the president ban them? What does it mean? *They tried to kill two presidents before. They tried to kill Nasser, and then they tried to kill Sadat. They did kill Sadat. People like them killed Sadat. Mubarak is scared they will kill him too, so he is being iron-fisted now that he's president. Iron-fisted means strict.* I nod my head. *The Brotherhood hate the president. They are violent and want Egypt to be like Iran.* I ask about Iran. *It's a dark place with no freedom. The number of women now wearing the veil is a red flag.* Mama is also scared of the women with scarves on their head. Dido nods. *Egypt never used to be like this.* But Baba told me before that nothing would change because Egyptians like to have a good time. Dido laughs. It's possible, he says. He tells me that next year the president will be elected again for his second term and he wants to make sure the Brotherhood can't challenge him. I look at him. *It's like a race, and the president is cheating in his own way so that he can win.* Who does he want to win? Neither. He thought Mubarak might be different but already he is proving he is just an old scrounge. I tell him Baba called the president a pharaoh. And he also said the pharaohs invented dictatorship. Dido laughs loudly.

Dido is a communist. It means he keeps to the left. He goes to meetings downtown and they talk about books. Baba said it's dangerous to be a communist. The government doesn't like them. It takes them away like all the other people we know. One of Baba's friends from school was in prison for five years because he was a communist. He wrote in a newspaper and the president didn't like what he said. He was twenty-three. When Baba told us the story we were at the beach in Alexandria sitting outside Granny's cabin. He was laughing and said nothing would ever change.

Look. He pointed across the bay to where Nasser and Sadat's cabins were and shook his head. Don't forget we had two revolutions, he told Dido. 1952 but also 1919. They came and went and all their hopes were shattered. Dido wore a communist-colored necklace and read books that Baba said could get him in trouble. He said he wasn't scared and that the revolution would come one day. I heard the word *revolution* all the time but didn't know exactly what it meant. Nobody answered me when I asked.

We cross the street. Dido points to a small square in the newspaper and tells me that our first president is sick. He has been living in isolation for thirty years. *Why?* Because life is unfair. We walk past the fruit shop where Mama buys our fruits. She calls by phone. They bring the fruit home in brown paper bags that tear at the bottom. The price is on the bag written with Biro. Today there are bananas, tangerines, watermelons, and melons, the green kind, like Baba likes. They are piled like pyramids on the pavement. The fruit man holds up one side of his galabia. In the same hand he has a black bag with his money. He smiles and gives me a banana. He asks if Baba is back. He calls him Bey. I shake my head. He points to Dido's newspaper. *Anything new?* There is a picture of the president on the front page at the top. It is the same picture every day. On the front page at the bottom there is a picture of the president's wife. Everyone calls her Mama Suzanne. It's what they tell us on television. A girl in school said she wanted to be like Mama Suzanne. I told Mama. She told me to wash my mouth with soap. I got up. I started to walk slowly towards the bathroom. Mama shouted that she never wanted to hear me say Mama Suzanne again. All my cousins call her Mama Suzanne. Nobody tells them anything. Every morning at assembly they sing the national anthem and then say, *We love Baba and Mama Suzanne.* At our assembly we only sing hymns. Dido is the only one who doesn't call her Mama Suzanne. Uncle says he is rebellious and doesn't understand how he turned out that way. Dido looks at the paper. He whispers but I hear him. He says a bad word. I eat my banana.

Dido takes the peel. He tells me that his life is politics and he hopes mine will be too. I look at him. We start walking. He takes a deep breath and says no one will ever compare to Nasser. He was a real man and one of the people. Baba also likes Nasser even though he made mistakes. Mama doesn't. She and Baba would sometimes fight. They would only ever fight about Nasser and money. Mama would scream about all the things that Nasser took from Grandpa.

Baba shouted back that he gave *his* father his *whole* life. Mama would say Uncle's name and that it was all about *wasta*. Connections. When I asked Mama why she was upset she took me to the window and told me to look out. Our street is long and filled with flame trees. Only one tree has purple flowers but only a few. The jacaranda . At school we learn that the British brought it to Egypt to make the country more beautiful. At night people paint bad words on the walls of buildings. In the afternoon men come and paint over them with black. Mama pointed to the red villa and asked me if I saw it. *Yes.* The white villa on the corner. *Yes.* The villa across the street that's a school. *Yes.* Her friends used to live in those villas, then Nasser took them, and they had to leave. Where did they go? They left the country. They packed their bags and left at dawn. They didn't even say goodbye. Was she sad? Very. Mama lost many friends because of Nasser. Her best friend was the daughter of the king and had to leave. Her other best friend was Jewish and also had to leave. Why did Nasser make them leave? Because life is unfair, and it was something I would have to learn. I looked at her. Mama had green eyes that changed color sometimes. I always looked to see what color they were. Baba told me once that if they were brown,

I should keep away. I asked her who would teach me about life being unfair. She said time.

We stop at the *foul* shop on the corner. The walls are tiled white like our bathroom. Dido lifts me onto a stool. There is a thin wooden counter to eat on. I put my hand on it and it sticks. I ask for a tissue. The man gives me a piece of newspaper. I wipe the paper on the counter. The sticky part turns black. Dido shakes his head. He turns back and asks the man for three sandwiches. And two bottles of Sinalco. Mama never lets me drink it. It is bad for my insides. It will turn them orange. Dido says Mama is too strict. *But without discipline I would become listless like the others.* He gives me a sandwich and sits next to me. Discipline can go either way, he says. It's the country that makes us listless. I ask him what *listless* means. It means to wake up every day and not know what to do. It means to feel there is nothing to look forward to in life. He laughs. Except football. I watch him. He takes a bite of his sandwich and stuffs a pickled carrot in his mouth after it. He looks at the street. There is a small blue pick-up truck with policemen on it. They are dressed in white. In winter they wear black. They jump off the truck outside the *foul* shop. A woman is sitting on the pavement with two baskets in front of her. One basket has tomatoes. The other cucumbers and lettuce. She tries to get up quickly but trips. She is wearing a colored galabia and has a large scarf around her head. One policeman takes her elbow. He pulls. The other takes her two baskets. He throws them onto the truck. She screams. What is she saying? Dido is staring at them and doesn't answer. People in the street stop and watch. Two cars stop. Four. Five. The traffic stops and cars behind start honking. There is shouting. One policeman pushes her into the truck. She screams, *Yalahwee*. He gets in after her and slams the door. The other policeman puts one hand on the back of the truck and jumps onto it. There is more shouting. More. They drive away. Dido shakes his head. The people who were watching walk away. The stopped cars go. Dido says a bad word. I ask him why they took her. He says the system is wrecked. And she doesn't have a permit. They don't give people a chance at an honest living. Why didn't he help her? He doesn't say anything for a long time and then shakes his head. He takes another bite of his sandwich. I watch him. He chews slowly, still shaking his head. After a while he asks if I remember what he taught me about the waves. I nod. *If it's going to hit me in the face I have to dive under it.* He raises one eyebrow and tells me to remember that in life too. He takes our sandwich wrappers and scrunches them into a ball. He puts the empty bottles on the counter. He gives the man five piastres. The man puts his hand to his head and salutes him. He calls him Basha.

I ask if we can get mango ice cream from El-Abd. Baba used to take me every Friday after school. He pats my head and takes the purple backpack from my shoulder. We walk to the curb. Three cucumbers are squashed on the pavement. I press on one with the tip of my shoe. Cucumber seeds squirt from one side. Dido raises his hand. A black and white taxi stops. *Downtown.* He opens the back door. I slide across the leather chair. It's boiling and I sit on my hands. Dido gets in the front next to the driver. He puts my bag between his legs and rests his elbow on the window. His arm hangs out. The driver has his arm the same way. Their arms might get cut off by a speeding car, but I don't say anything. The driver has a long nail on his little finger. Our driver also has a long nail on his little finger. So does the man who sells fruits. Their nails are even longer than Mama's. I imagine taking scissors and cutting them off. Dido talks to the driver. I move closer to the window and stick my head out. The taxi goes towards the bridge where the billboards are. Two men on ladders are carrying buckets of paint. Two other men are dipping their paintbrushes into the buckets. One of them is painting the head of a woman. Her dress is blue with white dots and the top of her breasts show in the way Mama says is not for my age. He paints yellow streaks onto her brown hair. The other man is painting a word. The taxi driver slows down. He shakes his head. *When are they ever going to finish? They have been painting the billboard for three weeks now.* Dido tells him it's an art. The poster will be up for years. The driver flicks his head. They talk about time moving at a pace of its own.

I listen to them with my head out of the window. Two women in short dresses come out of Simonds. They are wearing high heels and have bags on their arms. Their hair is up like Mama's. They have dresses like Mama's. They have necklaces like Mama's. They look different. They are laughing and throwing their heads back. I remember when Mama looked like them. They walk to the edge of the street and stand talking. I look back at them. We pass a new building. There used to be only two buildings on the Island. Then people started building everywhere. It's not what it used to be. Everyone is always saying that. That's why our house is special. Now they are even building a bridge. There are piles of sand and bricks and big trucks every night, and Mama complains about the noise. On TV they tell us the president will build five new bridges. Mama calls it a catastrophe. I try to imagine the island still just fields and houses. The taxi is the car like Grandpa had, white with an open top. He would take Mama to Simonds, but the one downtown, and they would have *bombe glacée*. It was a famous ice cream that they didn't make anymore. Mama said it was something of the past. Everything is of the past.

At home Dido sits on the sofa where Mama sits. It's Baba's place. I sit on the armchair next to him. He picks up the blue address book from the table. He turns it over. *It's Baba's.* He looks at me and puts it down. It's hot. I get up and turn on Granny's fan. Dido asks about Mama's plant mister on the table. I hand it to him. He sprays himself and says he loves the house. It makes him sad now. He misses Granny's lunches. I ask him where Mama went. He puts his elbows on his knees and leans close to me. He mists me. I squint. We laugh. Mama had some business to do. Does he miss Baba? Of course, just like me. Let's watch TV, he says. I get up and switch it on. There is a documentary about Egypt on Channel One. Dido tells me to leave it on. I frown. *But it's always documentaries.* He stares at the screen. First there are pictures of the king. He is standing on a boat holding a baby. The queen is next to him. She is dressed like Mama and doesn't look like a queen. They are leaving from Montazah Palace, where we used to go in the summer. All of Montazah Gardens used to belong to the king, Dido says. That's why '52 was good. It gave the gardens to the people. If there had been no revolution our summers would be different. Alexandria would be different. I ask again. *Revolution*. What does it mean? You could say it means change. Do Mama and Baba think it was good? It's complicated. Mama told me the story once but I forgot. He tells me the story. *The revolution happened in the summer. Granny and Grandpa would move from Cairo to Alexandria. The whole government would move to the coast during the summer months. It was too hot to be in the city. Mama, Granny, Nesma, and all the family would be there. They would go to the beach while Grandpa was at work. Grandpa was a judge in the royal court. It was very early in the morning when the revolution happened. Mama was on the balcony having breakfast. They heard a rumble from far away. Minutes later they saw army tanks. They went by right under their balcony, right along the corniche and towards Montazah Palace. Granny and Grandpa both said a prayer.* I remember that part. Mama told me that she could tell from their faces that something bad was happening. She doesn't remember anything else except that the summer ended suddenly. Dido says the revolution was bad for people like Grandpa because it took things away from them. But how come they didn't take our house when they took all of Mama's friends' houses? *It's just one of those things.* Mama says the house is the only thing we have left. Dido doesn't say anything. I love the house but I liked it better before, I say. *Before what?* Before it became so empty. Before everyone died and Baba left. Before people stopped coming and everything changed. He looks at me. Is that a revolution too? I ask.

Dido turns to the TV. They are showing pictures from inside a museum. The camera shows two glass cabinets. Opera music plays. One display has fields, mud huts, donkeys, men in galabias, women with big dishes on their heads, children playing in the canal. The other has roads and nice buildings and a red bus and men dressed like Baba. The camera zooms close to the writing on the displays. What does it say? I can't read so quickly. He reads. *Before the revolution. And*—he unzips his jeans—*after the revolution.* I watch him. He gets up and starts to pull them down. He says the house feels like a furnace. He doesn't re-member it being so hot. I stare at him from the side of my eye. He is wearing shorts underneath. Blue ones with pink stripes. I turn my head and look. There is a man outside the school who also unzips his trousers but he has nothing underneath, I say. When did this happen? He is there on many days. Have I told Mama? I shake my head. Why? I am scared she will get angry. He tells me I shouldn't tell anyone and that it's very bad. He will take care of it. I also saw something else. I saw my girl cousin kissing another girl on the mouth. Is it bad? He tells me it's not a secret but I should never talk about it to anyone. I nod. Why do they always play the film about the war on Fridays? Because everyone is watching TV waiting for the football match. They want people to remember and to forget. What do they want us to remember? How we won in 1973. What did we win? We crossed the Suez Canal and won back the Sinai from Israel. What do they want us to forget? About 1967. I already know about the Naksa. It was the war Baba wanted to fight in. He thought we were winning but then he looked up at the sky and knew. What did he know? That we had lost. That the president had lied. Why did the president lie? To protect us. When I asked him how he knew we had lost, he said the Israeli planes were flying right over his head. How did he know they were Israeli? The blue star. Baba said that day changed everything.

. . .

Every Saturday the two men would come to the house. They would ring the bell twice. The first time they came Mama was still asleep. I looked out of the window. They were wearing safari suits. The kind the president wears when he opens factories. They had papers in their hands. When they saw me they called *little girl* and asked for Baba. He hasn't come back. Mama? She is still sleeping. Can you come down and take these papers? I'm not allowed. I put my head back in and closed the window. I went inside and spied on them from the bathroom. They stood at the gate for a long time. When Mama woke I told her. She shouted and said I should never open the window by the door again. She picked up the phone and dialed a number. She spoke French. I stood at the corner of the doorway watching. She talked for a long time then put the phone down loudly. Get dressed, she said, and went into her bedroom. Her red silk robe was open and the sash fell to the floor. I rushed to pick it up. She closed her door. I stood with it in my hand and waited. There was no sound from her room. After a while I rolled it and put it on the floor. I moved it to the right to make sure Mama would see it when she came out. I went to my room and looked out of the window. The street was empty but I could hear the street sweeper. He had a straw broom and you could hear him on weekends and in the middle of the night. I changed out of my pajamas into red trousers and a white T-shirt. I put on white socks and my favorite blue shoes. I had three pairs of shoes. I went back outside and sat on the sofa. I waited with my hands on my lap.

Time passed slowly then the doorbell rang again. Mama came out. *Go to your room.* She had a visitor. I went. My room used to be Mama's room until she turned sixteen. After that they gave her a bigger one. It used to be blue, but Mama let me change it. I chose mustard. It was a strange choice for a young girl, Mama said. The color was different now. Darker. I wanted to change it again but Mama said I had made my choice and that it was a fact of life, *things get darker.* I stared at her.

I lie on the floor and stick my head under the bed. I open one of the hidden albums. The pictures are black and white but I imagine them in color. The first is of Granny at the door of the house. Her fur is slipping off her shoulders. She is standing with three women looking at the camera. Someone is kissing her. Here is Granny with her English friends. And the woman with the big pearls. Her lips look black in the picture but I know they are red. This one, Granny is surrounded by people. Everyone is listening to her. They are frowning like Mama tells me not to. This picture, my favorite, at the dining table. Everyone is laughing. Granny is talking to them with her hands in the air. Some pictures but not many have Grandpa. He is wearing a tarboosh. In one of the pictures it is colored red. In another picture his eyes are colored green, like Mama's. Mama tells me that she took Grandpa's eyes. They contained in them secrets like the sea. My eyes are different. They are dark like Baba's and you can't see into them. There are six pictures of me. Square ones with a white frame. Three of them are from the same day. In one picture Baba is carrying me on his arm. I am holding my bear, Fluffy. In another Mama has me on her lap. Then Aunty is carrying me with both arms. These pictures are colored. I'm wearing green pajamas. Baba, Mama, and Aunty are all in black. We are in the garden. Aunty has on dark glasses. I asked Baba once to tell me what happened that day. It was the day Uncle Hussein died. He was Mama's brother-in-law. They had just come back from burying him and were in the garden. Baba said he remembered the day like it was yesterday. It was the day Sadat made peace with Israel. He wished Uncle had lived to see.

After they killed Sadat, Baba stopped talking to *his* uncle, Ashraf, for a whole year because Uncle's son was one of the killers. He said it was his fault for not paying close enough attention. I heard him say that if he hadn't spent all his time with a glass in his hand, things might have been different. But nobody spends all their time with a glass in their hand. How would they sleep? I was scared Uncle Ashraf might be a killer too. Baba said I shouldn't be silly. It was just a trend with young people who were lost. They turned to religion. When he wanted to fight in the war, was he one of them? He laughed and said they were different things. Baba's cousin was still in prison for killing Sadat. He would be there for the rest of his life. It was a different prison from the one we went to when we saw Mama's thief. Nobody could go to this prison. They did terrible things to people there. More terrible than we could imagine. They tried to break people's souls. Baba said sometimes there was little difference between the living and the dead. His cousin might as well have been dead.

I stand in front of my mirror. I pretend I have flowers in my hair. I smile and twirl around. I'm in a field, on a hill. I open my mouth and sing without sound. There is a small picture of Mama when she was a girl on the mirror. I also have a picture of Baba carrying me. Grandmama says my relationship with Baba is special and no matter what, I should know that he loves me. She said Baba's *situation* is very common and many people were going through the same thing. I hear a loud sound. I open the window and stick my head out. There's a truck at the corner. Men next to it are planting yellow flowers around one of the trees on the side of the road. Others are painting the pavement. One is painting black. One white. They move forward, slowly. I watch. Paint. Plant. Plant. Paint. They are the only people on the street. It's Saturday. Nobody goes out on Saturday in the summer until the sun goes down. The streets are quiet, then at prayer the men come out. They walk to the mosque. When the prayer finishes the women and children come out too. It is cooler by then. Many people go to the club. The club also used to belong to the king. Then Nasser came and gave half of it to the people. He made it free. Half the fields and half the horse-racing track and half the golf course. The other half is for other kinds of people, like us. We have to pay. In the summer when we came back from Alexandria we would sit at the club with Baba under the eucalyptus trees and order a jug of lemonade.

I watch the truck move until it's right outside the house. Mama comes in. What am I doing? I point. They never paint the pavement or plant flowers. It's because the president's wife is coming to open the library at the end of our street. It's the most beautiful villa on the island. It used to belong to the Karassos, she says. Last time when the president was coming to the Opera House they did the same thing. Mama tells me, *Come on, we are going out for a while.* Where are we going? Out. Where? To buy fabric. For what? The armchair. From where? Downtown. How come?

In the morning Uncle came. He brought the newspaper and sat *plonk* on the sofa without kissing anyone or saying hello. *Look at this. They are floating it, but no doubt they will adopt it.* He put his finger on the front page then threw it onto Mama's coffee table. It slid and landed in the gap between the leg and the couch. I was standing by the *mashrabiyya* doors that lead to the bedrooms. Mama had been in the kitchen and walked in. She had on her reading glasses and looked at Uncle from over them and down her nose. Mama didn't like things lying on the floor. I picked it up. Uncle came every Sunday after Baba left. He wasn't really my uncle but we called him that. What are they floating? Mama asked. He waved his finger. *The flag.* I stared at the flag. It didn't look so different. *You see, if they approve it we're going to have to reprint everything. Everything, everything. It will cost the coun-*

try a fortune. All this for what? Ego! He made a sound like a huff, as if he were running. Uncle was always talking about ego. Before Baba left he told him that his problems were because of ego. They looked serious. I could tell it was an adult conversation. Uncle was at the house a lot before Baba left. They would go into the dining room and close the doors and talk. It was always night when he came and I would go to bed before they finished. Now Uncle came in the mornings. Always on Sunday.

The flag was like the old flag, with three stripes. Black on the bottom, white in the middle, red on top. It also had a golden eagle, but the eagle in the new flag looked different. His wings were different. They were bigger and had feathers. Uncle asked me to read. *Arab Republic of Egypt.* Did I know what the old flag said? It also said *Arab Republic of Egypt.* But it also said *Federation of Arab Republics.* The coloring on the new eagle was also different. Uncle had a big belly. You would see his belly before anything else. He looked at me and leaned forward. He was frowning. I couldn't understand why he was so upset. *You can say this is a modern eagle. An eagle for the times. Do you know how many flags we have had little girl?* The sweat was dripping down his head. There were puddles on his shirt. He kept looking at me. I shrugged my shoulders and shook my head. *Don't they teach you these things in school?* Uncle laughed heavily, also like Baba. *You know how many flags there have been? I'm sure even your mother doesn't know how many flags there have been.* He turned to Mama. *Of course not.* He laughed more heavily. *Please, one of you, an ice-cold glass of water.* Mama went. While she was gone he told me we had eight flags. This would be our ninth. It was testimony to how rich our history was. No other country had as many flags as we did. Mama came back with the water. She gave Uncle the glass. We watched. He drank it in one gulp then banged it on the table. Uncle never used the coasters and Mama picked it up quickly. I asked Uncle what the flags were. Mama said she would leave us to our history lesson. She went through the *mashrabiyya* doors to her bedroom. They were swingy doors but Mama never let them swing. She opened and closed them so that they wouldn't make a sound. Uncle asked me for a paper and my coloring box. I sat next to him. He began to draw. *These things no one will teach you.* Uncle drew well. He was an architect and designed houses. I liked drawing with him better than anyone else. He lived in a big house far away, in El Faiyûm, by the lake. His house was different from any other house. It had domes, like the kind in Aswan at the hotel we stayed in. Each dome had small holes, like windows, but tiny. Uncle said it was a cooling system. It was also about shadow and light. He told me that architecture was about making art as much as it was an exercise in finding practical solutions. Architects who thought like him were a dying breed. Uncle had studied with Hassan Fathy. People no longer designed and built the way Hassan Fathy did. He was eighty-four years old now and Uncle said *it's that time.* And only when he died would he be celebrated in Egypt. That's what Uncle said. I loved Uncle's house. Mama said it was too eccentric. Baba said it was too simple and not his style. He had a courtyard in the middle with a fig tree and a wooden bench. We would sit on it together and watch the shadows move. For one hour Uncle made me draw all the different shadows on a paper until in the end I had a drawing. He called it an abstract and told me it was a replica of a famous painting in a European museum. I can't remember which one. Everyone who had a house had a fig tree and an olive tree. They gave the house a longer life. The Quran said so. Granny planted four, but we only had two now. Mama said they were our protection. I could hear her in the bedroom on the phone. She took it in with her at night and brought it out again in the afternoon. Mama never sat with Uncle and me. She would wait until we finished drawing then tell me to go to my room because they had grown-up things to discuss.

Uncle was still drawing the flags. I liked the flag of Ottoman Egypt the most. It was red with a white moon and star. My second favorite was the Egyptian Revolution flag. It was a mix of three flags, including the one we used to have when we had a king. The ugliest was the United Arab Republic flag when we were one country with Syria. It looked like our flag now but with two green stars. One star was for Egypt and the other for Syria. Uncle said the idea of a United Arab Republic was a failed idea from the start. I looked at him. *Everything Nasser did was a failed idea.* I waited for him to say something else. He asked me for more water. When I came back with it, I asked him about Nasser. Dido says Nasser was a great man. The men who made the revolution were all great, but their children are corrupt. Nasser did great things for Egypt. Mama doesn't like him. Baba does. Dido hopes there will be another Nasser one day. How come they never tell us about Nasser at school? Uncle slapped his hand on his thigh. He had only finished half the water. The glass was on the arm of the sofa. He put it to his mouth and swallowed the rest. He put his arm out and I took the glass. Uncle started telling me about Nasser. *He had no vision. He was delusional. He didn't think into the future. He took from the rich and gave to the poor. It was the worst thing he ever did. The poor got things for free and then became lazy. They got land and lots of other benefits and then thought they could do nothing and Nasser would give them more. He also made education for free, which was very expensive, and so very quickly he didn't have the money to pay for it anymore. Education went down the drain. Teachers weren't being paid properly, so they didn't make an effort. Students had to start taking private lessons. Everyone stopped thinking. Everyone became lazy and stopped thinking. It was a lethal combination.* He paused to breathe. What does lethal mean? *To kill a country and its future. To destroy any opportunity for future generations. To take a beautiful field of flowers and pour concrete on it and still expect the flowers to grow.* I was always falling and hurting my knees on the concrete playground at school so I decided this must be bad. Nothing he did was sustainable, Uncle said. He took a big breath. Mama was always using that word. She used to tell Baba that his lifestyle was not sustainable. Uncle said we were still paying the price for Nasser's mistakes. But how come Dido said Nasser was a great man if he did so many terrible things? It was about education. At school they taught children that all the Egyptian presidents were great. Only the king was bad. Why was the king bad? Because he was a creation of the British.

Uncle asked if I ever went with Mama to the co-op. I nodded. Every week. Sometimes on Saturday, other times after school. The co-op was close to the house. It was like a shed on the pavement, a big shed. It was painted blue on the outside but the paint was peeling. You could see the wood. At the beginning of the month there would be a long line from the inside to the outside and onto the street. In the middle of the month it was emptier. The shed was lined with shelves. It was dusty. Sawdust covered the floor. They had bags of rice, flour, sugar, oil, boxes of tea. There were also frozen chickens, but they were in a freezer behind the counter. If you wanted a chicken you had to ask and a man would bring it out. He took your booklet. It was small, the size of the box of cigarettes hidden in the bathroom cabinet. In the front of it was Baba's name, Mama's name, and a number. A code for how much we were allowed of each thing. Sometimes people would try to take more than what they were allowed. They would raise their arms and shout. One man tried to take a chicken but wasn't allowed. You were allowed a whole chicken only if you were a family. Some people were only allowed half a chicken, so they could have one chicken every two months since they only sold chicken *by the one*. People shouted and tugged at their clothes. It was only the men who got angry. I would stand by Mama's side holding her hand. She never spoke to anyone. She would stand and look straight ahead as if nothing were happening.

They also sold bread, but you had to get it from a window on the side. I watched until I understood everything about the co-op. We were allowed five *baladi* breads a day. Uncle told us one day that bread was our downfall. People were taking their allowance and selling it to *other* people who wanted more. They sold it for much more than what they bought it for. Mama looked at him with her hands crossed on her chest. There is a black market for everything now, I heard her say. Uncle shook his head. *The catastrophe is the government employees are doing it too.* Some people couldn't get booklets because they didn't have birth certificates, and you needed a birth certificate to get a booklet. So what would those people do? *Black market.* Uncle said co-ops exist because of Nasser's mistakes. He bankrupted the country so it had to ration subsidized foods. Why can't they just sell things in a supermarket? He laughed loudly. *It would be a revolution. The country wouldn't survive another revolution.* But Baba said we had two revolutions and nothing changed. Baba said we need a real revolution. *Your Baba means a different kind of revolution. If the revolution were to come, it would be one of hunger, like the Bread Riots.* I looked at Uncle. They didn't teach us these things in school. Only Uncle and Dido told me. And Baba too, until he left. Mama said it was best to keep such thoughts to oneself, but Uncle never kept any thoughts to himself. He said that where he lived was like putting a finger on a pulse. Measuring a heartbeat. In El Faiyûm, where all the farmers lived, you knew what people would accept and what they wouldn't. If they stopped having co-ops, the farmers would go into the streets and start throwing stones and setting fires, like when flour became more expensive. It made bread more expensive. People revolted. *Those were the bread riots. This is the revolution of hunger. It was the year you were born.* Uncle put his hands into the sofa and pushed himself up. He put his hand on my hair and ruffled it. *You learned a few new things today.*

There was a picture of Mama and Baba's wedding on the wall. Every Sunday Uncle would stand in front of it and stare for a long time. Mama's hair was long then, it almost reached her waist. Baba had on thick glasses and sideburns. He was wearing a ring in the picture, but Mama said he took it off after the wedding and never put it on again. I asked where it was. Mama wasn't sure. Some days when she went out I would look through her drawers. I wanted to put Baba's ring under my bed with the albums. I also wanted to take something from his office but was scared Mama might notice. I went and stood next to Uncle and asked what he was looking at. I miss your Baba, he said. He squeezed my shoulder and told me to get Mama. They had business to discuss. I asked Uncle if he had been to Geneva. He bent his head down and frowned, then started laughing. What makes you ask about Geneva? Mama came through the *mashrabiyya* doors and told me to go to my room. I heard Uncle ask why I wanted to know about Geneva. Mama lowered her voice. I heard her say *Baba*. I didn't know why nobody talked about Baba even though everyone missed him. I still counted every day but didn't know anymore what I was counting to.

After Uncle left, Mama said we were going to the Mugamma. It was the biggest building in Cairo and everyone's papers were there. Mama had some business to take care of. The driver would be here in twenty minutes. I needed to make sure Ossi had enough water in his bowl. I needed to tidy my room. Was my bed properly made? We would have lunch when we got back. *What would we have? Could I help choose?*

Mama gave me a breadstick. She had on a dress the color of sand with a thin belt around it. She was wearing the sandals Baba had bought her when he met the famous Egyptian spy. They were from Hamburg. They were brown with many straps. Mama went down the steps. She told me to hurry and close the door behind me well. I sat in the back of the car next to Mama with the window down. We drove across the street named after the revolution towards the bridge. Mama stared out of the window. She was sad for Egypt. The driver slowed down. One of the big red buses had stopped. He stopped beside it. Its front was open and smoke was coming out. People were watching. Everyone had come off the bus. Men and women. A boy and girl sat on the side of the pavement with two plastic bags next to them. Women fanned themselves with newspapers. One man poured water from a bottle over his head. Some of the men were barefoot. I had asked Mama before how come people walked barefoot in the street. She told me it was a product of disillusionment. Then she explained. It was like looking at a painting and someone telling you that you see one thing, but you know that when you look, you see something else. Then every time they show you a painting, they do the same thing. You don't believe them anymore. After a while you stop caring. I listened. The driver started moving again. I asked if the bus was going to explode. I knew buses exploded. I crunched my breadstick. Mama turned her neck and watched as the crumbs fell onto my lap. She told me to be more careful. She looked away, and I brushed them onto the floor.

The bridge to downtown had two lions on each side. I gave them secret names in my head and whispered to them as we drove by. The lions guarded the Nile. They also protected the fishermen and their families who lived on boats as small as our bathtub. I imagined living in a bathtub. I asked Mama how they went to the toilet. She *tsssked* and made a face. Maybe the lions cleaned it up. On the other side of the bridge were two more lions. Beside them on a lamppost was a poster of the president. There were posters of the president everywhere. My cousins giggled when he came on TV. Dido made fun of them. He said the president was old enough to be their father. They didn't care. He didn't look old. Their dream was to marry a pilot and officer. The president used to fly planes in the war.

The Mugamma was shaped like a curve and had millions of windows. Uncle said that when it was built it was an architecture of hope. That was also something of the past. Mama told the driver to stay parked where he was. We would be out soon. We were double-parked next to a big black car. You weren't allowed to double-park but Mama gave the police money, then we could stay. We walked towards the big metal gates. People stared at us. There were policemen everywhere. Outside, inside. There were also men who looked like the Saturday men. Mama took my hand. She pulled me. We walked up the big marble staircase. It turned. We went up more. Then again. How many more floors? Come on. Is it far? Mama asked a policeman which way. He pointed. People were shouting. We walked. There were hundreds of doors. Policemen were sitting on chairs by every door. We kept walking. The corridor was long. It smelled like food. My feet hurt. I was hot. I looked into one of the offices. People had newspapers on their desks and were eating with their hands. I couldn't see what they were eating except for the bread. Everyone ate bread. They used it instead of forks or spoons. Mama shook her head. I was never allowed to use my hands. At the end of the corridor we turned left into a hall. There was a counter with many windows and people waiting in lines. They were pushing. People were always pushing. They pushed in the street. They pushed on the bus. They pushed at the co-op. They pushed in Port Said. When there were lots of people outside the shop near school they pushed there too. If you were tall it was better because you could stretch your hand over everyone and get what you wanted. I watch a short woman shaped like Grandpapa. She is wearing a red galabia and blue slippers with a white flower, like the kind we buy in Alexandria in the summer that break after a week and make Mama upset. A man who looks like a giraffe is standing next to her. His arm is stretched over everyone and he has it almost in the window. The line is meant to be one line but it's now three. People stick out from all sides. The red lady taps the giraffe man's hand. She nods with her head. He takes her paper. Both their papers are almost at the window.

Mama stood looking for a long time then took my hand again. She pulled at me towards the corner, where the blue door was. It had a gold sign. Two men stood on each side of the door. Mama whispered to them and brought out a paper from her bag. One of them knocked and opened the door. I saw chairs. A TV. The room was smoky. Everyone around us was smoking. The walls were dirty. The floors were dirty. People had scribbled and scratched their names on everything. A man, then another man, threw cigarettes on the floor. Only men smoked. Mama turned and looked. She pointed. *Sit.* I looked up at her. I couldn't see the color of her eyes. She nodded with her head again then turned and went inside. The door shut. The two men stood still like statues. I turned and shuffled to the chair. I knew Mama wouldn't be a minute. Baba used to say he would be a minute then I would sit and sit and it felt like time had stopped and he was never coming back. Sometimes people went to places and never came back.

I had come to the Mugamma with Baba many times. We made passports, we got my birth certificate, we made a special paper so I could travel with Mama without Baba. We also came once when Baba bought the land in the desert for the other house. When Granny died we came too. I didn't know what Mama was doing this time. I listened to people next to me talking about Zawahiri. One of them was looking at the newspaper. Two ladies put their hands on their chests and said *yalahwee. He should be in jail forever, and they've now set him loose on us. Yalahwee.* They kept talking but I stopped listening when the man came and sat next to me. He sat with his back straight up. I straightened mine. He took off his slippers. He rolled and unrolled the papers in his hands. He had a small beard like Baba's when he didn't shave. But he was thin. His shirt was wet. He turned to me but didn't say anything. I looked down at my hands. I could hear his paper rolling again.

When Mama came out I had a bottle of 7-Up in my hand. She asked where I got it from. I pointed. The man with the beard. I'm not supposed to take things from strangers. But it was so hot. You were gone so long. He gave it to me. I said I can't and he said I had to. Mama started walking. I got up quickly. I left the bottle on the floor. I followed her. The driver was waiting. *To the house,* Mama told him. She was exhausted. She would need to nap before lunch.

I put the fan on in the living room while Mama napped. I was allowed TV as long as it couldn't be heard. They kept playing Quran, then Mama Nagwa came on. Mama Nagwa was always talking about Mama Suzanne. She was also always telling us what was good and what was not. She told us we had to read. Children weren't supposed to talk a lot. We had to thank Baba and Mama Suzanne for all the good things they gave us. We had to love our teachers. I got up and turned to the other channel. A silent film. I stood by the TV with my finger on the panel. I changed back to Channel Two. Still Mama Nagwa. Channel One. Film. Channel Two. Mama Nagwa. I look at the door to Baba's study. I go to the kitchen. I take a chair and drag it to the counter. I stand on it and reach for a glass. I bend my knees and put the glass down on the counter. I push it so it slides back near the wall. I get off the chair. I drag it back to the table. I get my glass and fill it with water from the tap. The English girl in my class says tap water is dirty. It's from the Nile and will make you sick. Her mummy says. I told her what Grandmama said about the Nile water and promises. She made a face. I drink my water and make a wish.

I open the balcony and go outside. The streets are empty. I look next door. Every single balcony. Every single window. They are all closed, with their shutters too. When the shutters are closed in Nana's house it's dark. Even with the lights on, it's dark. I think that maybe for my next story for school I will write about the Dark People who live with their shutters closed. Mama likes to close the shutters when it's too hot. It helps keep the house cool. Baba said it's rubbish, but he let Mama close them when she wanted. In my bedroom the shutters only go down halfway. They broke a long time ago and nobody fixed them. Mama said she had to remember to phone the man to come and look at them. I told her it didn't matter. I didn't want the man. It means it never gets dark.

I go back inside. Channel One. Football. Every day there is football. Football is the people's oxygen,

Baba said. They have nothing else. The team that lost last time started fighting. The police took them away. We watched on TV, Baba and I. It was the day he told me I had to remember what people had been through. When you have a dream and someone makes promises they keep breaking, it is hard to recover. You lose hope. That was the day Baba told me I was luckier than many people, and no matter what happened, I had to remember that.

Football is boring. I go to my room. I look out of the window for a long time and imagine there is nothing there. Just the grass, like Mama said it used to be, and a sandy slope down to the river. It's ages since Mama's nap. I'm hungry. I finished coloring and watched everything on TV, looked at the albums under my bed, played with Nesma's cards, stood in front of the mirror, pretended I was singing on stage, played garden, planted flowers all over my room. I now sit on the edge of my bed waiting. It's dark outside. I get up. I walk on my tiptoes to Mama's door. She doesn't like it when I wake her up. Most of the time Mama closes her door, but sometimes when she takes her siesta she leaves it open the size of a pea. I put my ear near the crack. I try not to breathe. Mama hears everything. She also knows everything, even when I don't tell her. Grandmama said it's how mothers are made. When

I become a mother I will understand. I told Grandmama there were too many things I was waiting to understand. She laughed and patted my head. She said it's better not to know too much anyway. I take one step closer and hear whispers. The phone is outside. Maybe Mama is talking to herself, like Uncle does. I stand for a long time then put my small finger on the door. It doesn't move. I'm scared it might squeak. Everything in the house squeaks. I suck my breath in and push again. I put my eye to the crack. Mama is on the floor. Sitting on her knees. She has a scarf on her head like Grandmama and the evil woman in the street. I stand as still as I can. Mama keeps whispering. After a while I hear my name. Then Mama says *Al Salam Alaykum.* I suck my breath deeper and tiptoe back to my room. Out of the window I see a small cloud. We never have clouds. I wish I could catch it and keep it.

PART TWO

SUMMER 1998, CAIRO

THE LINE OF ANTS EXTENDS from the neck of the toothpaste tube across the sink up the wall by the mirror and into a crevasse between two tiles. On television they have been warning about ants, these small black beady ones in particular. In a moment they can be all over you, and their bite, if a collective effort, can kill. So says the TV. Uncle insists it is a metaphor, that the regime is sending subliminal messages about the Islamists who have been staging sporadic bombings and attacks. He suggests I start taking notes, keeping a diary of phrases, creating an archive of messaging and making the connections. It could be a book, he tells me, or maybe a short film. I watch the ants for a few minutes considering the theory. It seems far-fetched. I also find it hard to kill the ants in the way the TV advises, filling a plant mister with medicinal alcohol and boiling water and spraying it over everything, *even the inside of your shoes*. I turn to the mirror. I twist and roll my hair into a bun. I button my jeans, faded Levi's with an *e* printed upside down. My navy T-shirt is oversized with a logo of a man on a camel playing polo. I put a long white cotton shirt over it, unbuttoned, sleeves rolled. I turn around and peer over my shoulder. I stretch out the bottom of the T-shirt so there's less of a silhouette from behind.

It's early, Mama wakes up late, but I knock, lightly, on her door each morning and whisper that I'm going down. Does she need anything? I leave a note on the fridge. I go down the back stairs and walk around the house to the street on the Nile. Billboards tower on the pavement advertising the new mobile phone company. Flyers for a new coffee shop are strewn on the tarmac, muddied by footprints. I take the bus. We lost the driver some years before, unable to afford the raise he requested, or to find someone who would work for less. We had lost most everyone, family first, then the large and varied staff that Granny had kept and Mama inherited. For all the sprawl of the house it was just me and her now, and a woman who came every ten days to clean. The house was like an echo chamber, most rooms kept permanently closed. You could hear the wind when it would come brushing even lightly against the old wood-framed windows. The floor continually squeaked. During the night inexplicable rumbles would wake me up. As a child, I had imagined these murmurs of the house to be tea parties on the roof. Now I wondered about the poetics of space, the cavities people once filled. Mama never spoke about how things had changed, but it hung heavily on her. I could see it in her gestures, how she sat at her dressing table each morning, ends of her hair in hand, combing, endlessly, as if treading in her own oblivion. Her hair was shorter now, there was little to brush through. Eventually she would come out to make breakfast. Mama drank her coffee black and ate just a quarter slice of toast with date jam. Some days I tried to make her coffee the old way, thick with sugar and cream, but she would look into the mug deeply as if she could see the bottom, then leave it untouched. The only days she made breakfast were the ones when Dido passed by on his way to work. She made him scrambled eggs and coffee the way she used to for Baba, putting *shatta* in the eggs and adding a spoon of salt to the coffee before mixing in five spoons of sugar. You didn't feel the salt, but it brought out the flavors.

I stand at a slight distance from the stop, looking

in on the garden and house as I wait, watching others peering in too. It is a maneuver to get on the bus. By the time it reaches this stop, almost at the end of a line to downtown, it is always full, windows open, heads sticking out, people dangling from the door, one foot in, one foot out, hands grabbing onto what they can. I let a first bus pass, then a second. When the third comes, I push my way in, sticking my twenty-five-piastre note through the crowds, crinkled, dirty. It's pulled from my grip, and a pink scrap is probed back into my palm. I scrunch my fingers around it and push. The last row is reserved for women, if they can find their way through the glut of men. I do. It's full, but one woman lets me stand close to her feet, offers to take my bag. I hold up my palm. *Thank you, it's okay.* She puts her hands to my hips and pulls me closer. I feel conscious of my groin almost in her face. She holds me there the entire ride. I try not to make eye contact. I focus on the conversations nearby about the heat. I hold my tense body as if relaxed, or unawares.

The route to downtown is one I've taken for years, around the perimeter of the island. Once a view of the Nile, of rowers plowing through thick waters in the morning, is now just fence, wall, fence, overgrown garbage-filled hedge, more fence, more wall. Dust coats it all like rind. Army clubs and government cafés take what space they can down to the banks, reserved only for those in upper executive ranks. The river is barely visible, except on one solitary stretch of a few meters where the hedge refuses to grow. Going to school we would drive down the island's length, then curve back to the eastern side. To university I continue, over the bridge with the lions and towards Tahrir Square. Police line it, slouched young conscripts leaning on loaded rifles. A man sits on the pavement selling roses. Another shining shoes. One swinging key chains. Leafy greens mark the spot of another vendor, who might have left earlier, or been taken away. They let some people stay. They take others away. Some are placed undercover.

I cross from one pavement to the next in the direction of the museum, looking right, across the square. Railings are being drilled into the tarmac, coated with enamel, painted black. The city's little green space is now fenced off, but the grass is dead anyway, the color of straw. I cross from one pavement to another around its edge. The overhead pedestrian walkway is long gone, torn down one day after my tenth birthday. Uncle had come to the house a few days later, a Sunday, newspaper in hand, complaining. Mama had been sitting on the sofa, I on a cushion close to her feet. There was never anything in the paper anymore except the bridges the president was building, the new cities, schools, libraries, hospitals he paid for. There was also the triple-outlined front-page daily box, untitled, listing phone calls and letters of praise from world leaders. It still existed, almost a decade later. Uncle had fallen into the armchair with a thud that day, dropped himself down, arms following, my eyes plummeting with him, catching his words. *A national monument has been destroyed.* He shook his head with rigor. I remember looking at him and thinking he meant the Pyramids, Mama's jaw dropping too. Then he launched into describing the most elegant circular walkway in the world, perhaps even the only one. Its proportions and elevation meant that no matter where you stood, you could see the entire green lawn of the circle in the square and the complete fountain and Italian-made sculpture. Nothing obstructed your view, regardless of what height you were at. Mama had picked up the newspaper to look for the story. Uncle groaned about the government's neglect, not even informing people that the square would be closed. He had driven into the city to attend a meeting honoring fifty-five years of the Egyptian Surrealists, held in a storied building just off the square, and as he approached, found it barricaded. Why? Because. Can't you at least put a sign up? He parked. A quarter of the walkway had already been demolished. The square was a mess, the lawn and fountain covered in rubble. It was just one of many acts of destruction, he had said, erasing the identity of a city. *Everything we ever knew will be gone. Anything with traces of past histories.* It was the legacy my generation would inherit, one of destruction and loss. He was sad for what we had been born into. *Tadmeer. Tadmeer.* It meant devastation. He worried it was who we had become. Sweat dripped off him like melted wax.

My memories of Uncle are the sharpest, most defined. Then, now. He complained about the walkway, and in my mind's eye, even as a child, it brought back the flag. He had been as upset about one as the other. As I walk through the square I see, hear, feel him. I relive past moments. With Baba, only the stories are left.

I take a step up onto the pavement, maneuver over broken tiles patchworked with tarmac and pockets of sand. The gates of the museum.

Egyptian?

Egyptian, you're sure?

Yes Egyptian.

Egyptian? But you pay less.

I nod. Pay the twenty-five-piastre ticket. Enter. Two girls in colored veils hold hands by Sekmet. A friend snaps a shot. They giggle. I walk past the last dynasties, the fake Rosetta, Thutmosis III, Thutmosis IV, Amenophis II, Hatshepsut, granite coffins, black cats, Ibis, the relief with part of Nefertiti, her head turned sideways. Kohl holders, carvings, relics piled almost atop one another, crammed in corners, onto shelves, on staircase landings. The museum smells like Granny's floor, musty, air trapped from decades earlier. I walk through, imagining the British looking for space, more space, trying to make sense of all they have found, creating labels, partial labels, incorrect labels. It's haphazard, disorderly, a relic from the time it was built as much as it is a work in progress. Students are clamored around one set of reliefs, drawing, putting papers onto exposed limestone and taking down rubbings. I hear the murmur of a young girl wanting to take home a beaded gold necklace. *Imagine if it were mine?* I find the statue of Akhenaton, the one where he is peering down, one hand on the shoulder of his young son. Black granite, alabaster eyes, lips pursed as if in motion, about to breathe. I sit cross-legged on the floor and bring out my notebook. I've taken to writing letters to people who don't exist or once existed or exist only as statues or gods. I've spent many hours by this statue, the only one of a pharaoh, a ruler, depicting love towards a child. The steely formalism of pharaonic sculpture was set aside in the case of Akhenaton, his humanism represented in gestures, expression, the lines of his face. My letters to A are obsessive, about who he was, how he inhabited his body, expressed love, came to find such conviction in his worship of the sun god Aton. *How did he deal with difference?* I want answers I know I will never get. *Dear Akhenaton,* I begin. I trace the outline of his body with my eyes. His breasts, his curved hips. I imagine him lying beside Nefertiti in bed, fingers tracing parts. In the margins of my notebook, I make note to read more about Nefertiti and her love for A. I write: *What does it mean to be devoted?* I underline these notes. I write *Nasser* beside them, circled, with a question mark. Notes I return to now.

Dido believes there is no space for real romance when we are fighting, but he wants his genes passed on. He wants the next generation to be comrades. We are too passive, he says, and have the capacity neither for revolution or for love. He uses a word, *poranheyar,* to explain our emptiness. A kind of devastation. Something passed on by the generation before. A word he invented, hybrid Arabic and Russian. There isn't a language for what we are living. We need our own vocabulary, not just new forms in literature and art. He is teaching himself Russian because he thinks that in their literature he might find answers, a language that speaks to all he feels about the politics of our times. He says this even though he doesn't write or make art, but he consumes everything, watches every film he can, reads and rereads novels, goes to every art opening, opera, play. He was the one who had put a VHS tape of Chris Marker in my hands and told me not to do anything else until I had watched it. Art is what sustains him, he says, gives him the energy to keep going. Dido takes down cases all day, oral histories of torture, abuse, arrests, at the hands of state agents. Even their emotions, these victims, what they are left with, the trauma, has no terms or designations. Nobody has a voice, he says, nor a real sense of who they are. He insists that the streets are simmering, filled with people's outrage, but our emotions are misplaced, making us silent.

I cross the square towards the university thinking about this, my next letter to A, how I will write to him about this feeling of being muted. Not having a language, gestural. How do you even initiate intimacy or the expression of desire? Mama never spoke about love. Nobody I knew who had ever really loved did. I imagined it was something Baba might have spoken of now. I turn the corner onto Mohamed Mahmoud Street. McDonald's opened a few weeks ago, and the queue, now, is immense. I peer above it to find its end, tracing heads around a corner. It was on the exact same stretch of street that Baba heard the engines of jets, looked up, and saw the Star of David, on his way to volunteer to fight in that very war. It was one of those markers in memory that he said never went away. I felt deceived too, cheated out of a life, but I wasn't sure why or by what. I wondered. Was that also inherited, our listlessness, sense of resignation? People, the older generation, Aunty and Uncle and all the others, would always somehow revert in conversation, even when talking about the price of food, to "'67." *Defeat, we are a defeated nation.* But even though Nasser had lied, people still wanted him to stay. They pleaded, took to the streets in millions when he resigned. Baba had spoken about that so often that even as a six-year-old, I could recite those stories by heart. They stayed with me. I had asked, *Why did you want him to stay, Baba?* He had stared into the air, looked around, then peered down at me. Raised his shoulders, his eyebrows, pushed his glasses up from the tip of his nose. He muttered something about heroism, then said he wasn't sure. He didn't have an answer for me. I write this down in my journal now, under the heading "Notes on Defeat", and beside an asterisk, a line about Uncle telling me years later that as a general rule in life, we act out of fear. We always choose what we know best, even if it means compromise.

I think about Baba more and more. At a point the idea of someone long absent turns from emotion into something of a mental exercise in remembering and deduction. The last time we were downtown together, Baba had described, wistfully, the cityscape during his student years. There had been little except villas, a few low-rise modernist buildings, and a palace ground divided. Open space was the city's marker. One of the three buildings that had always been there, once with its own garden, now encased on three sides with highrises, was the one where Abu Seif's studio had been. Baba had wanted to study film, but Grandpapa hadn't let him. Young men were to study finance, the only way to a respectable life. Either that or they went into the faculty of law. Baba couldn't argue with Grandpapa, so he skipped classes and spent days in the studio. He had been there when Abu Seif made what became his canonical film chronicling the aftermath of defeat. The only film from the time that Nasser hadn't banned. I think about this, Baba's activism, the person he might have been before he became a businessman. I have his university ID on my desk at home.

I stare into it. I remember certain things. The sound of his breath as he wound up his wristwatch. How he gestured with his hands as he spoke. His footsteps up the stairs, the long pause and then rattle as he brought out his keys. The movement of his face just before he broke into laughter. I can't imagine him interested in film. I hear things here and there, but no one says much. What I know about him I construct, piece together, through stories, notes, remembered dreams, interpreting recurring ones. A theater professor asks me one day why I have chosen the art form I have, why I have chosen art at all. And then he tells me his own story.

Dido urges me to involve myself in politics, to make documentary films about dissidents rather than the cinematic ambitions of fictional cinéma vérité I have. It's about time, he says, it's important to connect with my anger. He says I can make art through activism and documentary, a different art, more potent. But that's reality, not art. He is adamant, and becomes more insistent. Surprises me on campus between classes, gives me books inscribed and signed, *Please. Love.* He also passes by the house on odd Saturdays, bringing me ten piastres' worth of dried sunflower

seeds, sitting beside me on a step in the garden, blowing perfect smoke rings from rolled cigarettes. I listen
as he goes on about reform, and I start methodically
recording our time together, flipping my notebook
back and around and making that side for him. I start
each entry with his mood, writing down everything
I remember of our afternoons. He's the only person I
know who speaks of changing the country. Love and
revolution are one, he says, they come together. In the
past two years there have been gatherings of people
in the square with signs chanting for Palestine. Nobody ever mentions Egypt. People generally don't talk
about the status quo even though everyone yearns for
change. I do. It seems that politics is at the foreground
and background of everything yet not something that
can be impacted in any way. Mama wishes things were
different, though she never says so in direct ways. But
I can tell. Even when she smiles or laughs, I can see
her sadness is much greater, a melancholy so seeped in
who she is. I'm not sure anyone I know is deeply angry,
even as they are unfulfilled, restless, somewhat resigned. Uncle complains about things, laments, talks
about the incompetency of government, but not with
the vehemence of anger that Dido suggests. I don't
think I am angry at all, as much as Dido insists we all
are. He says we just don't know how to express it, that

we weren't taught to be in touch with ourselves. The way we live our lives is no better than death.

Sociology. The professor is showing us slides of different types of drugs. The most common is a form of cannabis grown in the Nile Delta. We had been with him on a field trip to Qanater prison the week before. The prison is divided. There is the new prison, with tiled floors and a TV and shaded courtyard, where the men are kept, and the old one, where the women are. At the prison gates families are waiting to visit. They come each day with food, clothes, medicines, begging the guards to let them in. The guards make them wait. Take their names, IDs, the names of their loved ones. They also take tips. It's no guarantee for entry. They still wait all day. Some spend the night. On the day of our visit, one woman is wailing. She's been waiting for three days in the searing heat. She came all the way from Qena, seventeen hours by bus. She is large and has on layers. Sweat pours from under her scarf. She screams. This is unjust, have mercy on me. The guard opens the gate to let us in. She tries to push through. We are the first people they've let in for days. I feel bad, almost guilty. Two men grab her and push her back. They are the same men I saw in the Mugamma, the same men who came to the house, the same men I see downtown now, standing at street corners, watching. We were let in to the main courtyard. It looked like a construction site, strewn with sand and rubble, littered, lined on one side with three-story buildings. Cigarette butts were everywhere. As we walked toward the low-lying visiting area, the whistles and shrieks began. I turned my head. From the windows, behind bars, I could see the women. They stuck their arms out. Their legs. Tongues. There was a clamor, and it was hard to make out what they were saying, each one. At one building galabias were lifted to expose bare bodies. A pair of breasts dangled from a window, squeezed between the bars. *The building is where the prostitutes are kept.* They are the least harmful of all the inmates, none of them have killed, none have cut their husbands into cubes, none have drowned their children. None fed poison to families. None murdered for money. *But they are the most disruptive*, the prison warden explained. One woman screamed that she wanted to drink us all. Suck us. She was thirsty. Her thirst could never be quenched. We looked delicious. Everyone turned away. I tried to stare at her without making it known, out of the corner of my eyes.

The clicking of the projector continues from the cannabis to the cocaine. The drug market is largely controlled by the state's security apparatus, the professor explains. It's convenient for the government that *foul* is the national food since beans make people sleepy. He laughs at his own joke. And that's why the government floods the market with cannabis. The street name is hashish. He tilts his head. *Between us,* he whispers in his Lebanese accent. I close my notebook and slip out. Down the long open hallway, around, down three flights of marble steps, to the other side of the building. Room 202. I'm early, always, and everyone else late. I take my seat by the door and bring out my thesis project, a film proposal. The title pays homage to a film by Jean Rouch and Edgar Morin. The filmmakers ask people on the street a single question one summer. *Are you happy?* I don't yet know quite what my question is, but know I want to set it in the summer. In my journal I write about wanting change. I have a cousin in America who left Cairo abruptly one summer. Something happened to him, but nobody speaks about what. I imagine myself in America. I think about the last summer before Baba left. The last summer we were all together. Mama saying that all she knew after the palace coup was that the summer ended quickly. Maybe I could ask people if they are angry. People seem disheartened. We all have frustrations, grievances, but anger? I watch them at sidewalk coffee shops, drinking tea, smoking, watching TV, for hours. They sit quietly, their faces blank. I imagine if they harbored anger, they wouldn't be so quiet. They wouldn't sit for so long. Their faces, expressions, would hang differently. I wonder, if I ask them, what they will say. I imagine they might fall silent. Feel uneasy. But if I keep rolling into the silence, will they fill it by talking about their lives? Or will they just get angry that I am asking? People get scared when you ask them things on the street. For a writing assignment we are asked to approach passersby with the question of what they would like to see improved in their city. People walked away. They looked at me skeptically. They asked who was asking. They asked who was really asking. They said they couldn't answer such questions. They put their hands up and shook their heads. They took steps backwards, sideways. They said they couldn't speak about the city. They couldn't speak about the country. Sorry. You know how it is. I don't want to get in trouble. I don't want any problems. So why are you asking exactly?

Habiba walks in and sits next to me. She flicks her hair to the right and shows me a dyed purple strand by her ear. The highest spiritual color, she says. I laugh and call it cute. She frowns. It's not cute. Don't use that word *cute* so freely. Not very much in this world is cute. I flip my page. She tells me it's for karma and good energy, then peers at my papers and puts her finger to a paragraph and laughs. Laughter back. She recognizes herself, in a character named Dido. She looks at me. Then says. You should write a novel, not a screenplay. How? Do everything you want with the screenplay but in the novel. It's easier. Less costly. You don't have to produce it. We spend the class playing word games on the margins of my pages, zoned out to the professor's reading of Albert Hourani. He reads aloud from chapter five. *Z broplem wiz z Arap world.* H rolls her eyes at me. We have twenty-one chapters yet to go. On the first day of the semester he had told us there were a few things we needed to know. *I am, from, the middle class*, he said. *My family had nothing. In the 1960s I studied hard at the university, and I was granted one of Nasser's bursaries to go to the United Kingdom to complete my PhD. Without Nasser I would have never had the chance to travel.* He said this as if standing atop a podium giving a public speech. His English is weak despite having studied in England and obtaining a PhD from Leeds. H and I laughed about this later as she mimicked him, sitting on a step after class, initiating the rites of passage to become friends. She rattled off a monologue mixing *p*'s and *b*'s, *z* for *th*. I am *z* lucky ones to have gone to *z* English school, I said. Then laughed, trying to earn her laughter too. Her reaction was fierce. The occupation was the worst for us. They were the dark ages. They took us back decades. My education undermined my identity. It broke my character. I should be furious that the British school even exists. I shouldn't even joke about it. She paused to catch a quick breath. I hesitated and didn't say anything but realized how much I liked her. *Wanted to be her?* We sat under the shade of a flame tree. She asked about my film. She talked to me about her major, physics, and then of her interest in artificial borders. She didn't buy anything made in Israel or America. Didn't drink coffee because the money benefits Israel. Doesn't wear certain kinds of shoes because the soles are made in Israel. Even the plastic cups in the cafeteria, they benefit Israel. Did you know? She doesn't use the term *Middle East* because it is a creation of the British. To use it is to remain colonized. I used *Middle East* all the time. I nodded and made a mental note to be careful.

I cross the paved courtyard towards the library. It looks like a giant slab of concrete with slim glass shafts. None of them open. The only fresh air into the building comes from the door. When I started university, one of the librarians tells me it is because of

Baba and his friends the new library is built this way. They used to throw books out of windows as students. I looked at the lady as she told me the story, not sure if I should believe her. She was wearing a dress with a lace collar and had on black sandals. Her body was soft. Her thick glasses were attached to a chain that sat on her shoulders and draped around her neck. On her dress I spotted a stain.

I sign out for my video equipment from the library's AV room. People watch me. There are only three film majors, and we are all, always, watched. I exit the campus. Passersby stare. The only people who are allowed to film on the streets are the TV. They work at the Egyptian Radio and Television Union. If you work there, you are also *the TV.* You are also, maybe, someone with ties to the surveillance state. Someone who it might be better to stay away from. I cross. On the old campus I go to the walkway between the basketball and tennis courts. The floor is paved with pink and yellow hexagonal tiles. I step only on the yellow ones. One step. Pause. One step. Pause. Sideways step. At the end of my path is the science building. I walk up the five steps at the entrance and set my tripod to the side. The university cameras are old, batteries last for less than twenty minutes before going out. I look for a power supply. A guard approaches me. He shakes his head. You can't set up here. But I'm on assignment. Sorry. But my professor asked me to. Sorry. But I'll fail if you don't let me. It's against the rules. Please. We can't allow it. But I have permission. Show me your permission. Here.

You can't be?

I look at him. He peers as if into my face, through it, eyes wide. His silence like a gasp. He had known Baba. He sets up my power. Asks if I need anything. What a great pleasure to meet you. Your Baba was a great man. If ever you need anything. *Anything at all.* I adjust the camera. I hit record.

The first sit-in I witnessed was eight months ago, last winter. A silent sit-in, candle-lit. It was the first political act on campus. University guards had hovered in the distance and then come closer, but they seemed unsure what to do. I also watched from afar. No one would talk about it at first except in whispers. H called it *the thing.* Then the government daily *Al-Ahram* ran a piece. Accompanying pictures showed three young men in black T-shirts, leather straps on their wrists, one of them with dreadlocks. It went: The American University encourages disobedience. It's the nesting ground for a new and dangerous movement. They take drugs and engage in sexual acts. They worship the devil. They practice homosexuality. They might have AIDS. The sit-ins are part of a larger movement of disobedience. They believe in anarchy. A Nirvana album cover runs alongside. Suddenly everyone is talking about it. The journalist is campaigning to get the university shut down. H calls on the home phone one day soon afterwards to say we are in for excitement. She has done some research. The same journalist wrote a piece a few years ago about young rockers. He described them as atheists. Then one night, without warning, the police had spread across the country banging down doors, dragging over a hundred young men from their bedrooms in the middle of the night. For three months they disappeared. Nobody knew where they were, if they would resurface. Parents searched and asked in vein. Lawyers were told to keep away. Ninety-seven days later they showed up, all of them, knocking on the doors of their homes. They wouldn't speak about what happened. Nobody dared to ask. Scars peered from necklines and sleeves.

I don't know what might happen this time but anticipate something. H's excitement is my fear. Maybe they will storm campus and arrest students and take them away. But who will they take? How will they know who to take? What will they do? We wait. I wait. I imagine. It shames me, this cowardice. Nobody comes. Men loiter in the streets around campus. They dress normally, simply, in plain clothes, but I know, we all know, who they are. They stand around. They look. They talk on phones. They never bother us. But they are there. One day I hear that a girl has been arrested for drugs. I don't know if they caught her outside the university. I don't know if she was caught by these men. Nobody speaks of it aloud, only whispers, rumor. I look to see where they are before I cross the street. I don't want to cross paths. A friend of Dido's is grabbed and taken away crossing their path, walking towards them unaware on his way to a café. I begin to wonder what happened to the man who worked for Uncle Mohsen, and the boy who cleaned cars at the garage next door. He never came back. I look at his parents and siblings each time I walk by and wonder if they know, or still have hope. Were there answers, or had they already said final goodbyes? I look around, my eyes darting, searching.

I focus my camera on the sit-in. The organizer talks into a loudspeaker, thanking everyone for coming. He is pleased with the turnout despite the summer. There are forty-one, forty-two, forty-seven students there. He takes out a folded paper from his back pocket. A

black and white Palestinian *kūfiyyah*, circles his neck.
Everyone claps. He makes a peace sign and reads:

> *BismAllah Al Rahman Al Rehim, God the Almighty the Merciful,*
>
>   *On July 2, Mohamed and Rana Abdel Jaber had their home destroyed for the second time in twenty-seven days. The invaders sounded an alert giving them five minutes to evacuate their home that had just been rebuilt. They lived in two modest rooms. Their life savings had gone into building this home, and then rebuilding it again. They took their three children all under the age of six and fled. They are now in a white tent that looks just like this. They are among tens of thousands of Palestinians displaced by Israeli forces. These acts of brutality and murder must end.*

I zoom with the camera and notice the son of the
Palestinian poet Mourid El-Barghouti, a poet himself. I pan. I don't know him but recognize his face.
Their story has been in the papers; Sadat deported
Mourid on the eve of the signing of the peace treaty
with Israel, and their family had lived separated for
seventeen years. I've devoured his wife's novels. The
poet wrote that it was the reason he had only one son,

otherwise he might have had eight. It was his fate for marrying an Egyptian. They had finally been reunited a few years ago, on pardon from President Mubarak. Mourid had returned to Cairo. I focus on his son's face, this only child of circumstance, wondering if I can script him into my graduation film. Then I move my lens out to take in the girls nearby. The chanting is insistent. Voices loud. Faces animated. I see determination. Sincerity. A glimmer of sadness. In the end, all I really see though is chatter. I think that's what I see. I film until I sense I have enough.

I sign the equipment back. Walk down the library steps. Enter the reserves room. It is really a storage closet lined with shelves. A man in a sweat-drenched shirt stands behind a wooden counter. The library is air-conditioned, but this closet is not. 301.H. The man doesn't acknowledge me but walks to a shelf. Pulls out a folder. Opens it. Brings out the papers. Waves them. The assigned chapter for philosophy class. *Fifteen piastres.* I nod, give him twenty-five, take the papers. Some students buy actual books, most of us photocopy. He puts the money in a cardboard box below the counter, then turns and rummages in a folder. I exit and turn the corner. Past the mango stand. The shop that sells under-the-counter beer. The man who sells matches and Adams chewing gum and plastic combs off a cardboard crate turned sideways on the pavement. A little girl runs to my side and hop-skips next to me. She holds a packet of tissues into my chest. *Fifteen piastres.* May God be generous. *Ten. Only ten. Ten.* I have only enough for my bus fare and a few things from the grocer that Mama needs. *Five. Five. Just five.* Sorry. *Anything. Anything to make my day.* She pleads. I'm sorry. She tugs at my shirt. I walk. Please take one for whatever you want. I shake my head. She tries to put her hands around my waist. I keep walking. Please. I shake my head. Please. I walk and say nothing, her hand still on my waist. We get to the corner where the bus stop is. I walk to the glut of people waiting for number twenty-nine. She follows me. I stand. She stands next to me. I say nothing. I look ahead. Eventually she goes away.

At home Mama has the shutters closed for the heat. The fan is on. The TV is on with volume. The washing machine is rumbling in the background. When I come back in the afternoons, I never know what I might find. There will either be the chorus of domestic sounds, or complete silence. Mama is nowhere. I push through the *mashrabiyya* doors and see her bedroom closed. I knock gently and pause. I stand for a minutes. Strain my ears. Lean my body forward. I wait a minute more, then go into the bathroom. I undress. My clothes fall into a heap on the floor. I roll my hair into a bun. I stand under a lukewarm shower. The water turns from gray to clear. When it turns to a cold trickle, I turn it off. I hear Mama through the door. I wonder what she does. She doesn't speak much about what's on her mind. I don't ask. She doesn't ask. The unasked questions feel heavy between us.

In my bedroom I stand over my desk looking out of the window as I towel-dry my hair. My drawer is open, crammed with notebooks, and drops of water fall into it and onto an open journal. They are heavy enough to make a sound. The paper quickly shrivels, and the ink spreads. I pass time outlining the blots of ink, then braiding and unbraiding my hair.

After a while the home phone rings. I go outside and pick it up. It's H. We had made plans to go to the cinema but canceled because her father had been glued to the TV and said he had a bad feeling. Not all the channels could be wrong, and all of them, *fifteen,* were saying the same thing. The fundamentalists were going to bomb cinemas. It was just a matter of time. I stand on one foot speaking to her, watching through the French doors as Mama prunes her plants by the window, muttering to herself. Sometimes she seems to be reprimanding people from her day, other times reciting prayer. Mama had started praying more after the earthquake. She believed in God, whatever *He* chose for her would be right, but she still worried about things. Being in the wrong place at the wrong time. Death. Making sure she didn't tempt fate. We were in the kitchen when it happened. The sky had fallen dark then turned red, and the house began to shake. Mama screamed and leaped up from her chair. I froze. She grabbed me. Suddenly we were standing in the middle of the room, glasses rattling, cutlery flying from the table, food sliding across the tile floor. Mama held me tighter than she had ever held me before, reciting the *Shahada*. She might have kissed my head. Her version of the story is less dramatic, except that she thought it was the end of the world and was saying prayers for both of us. Later that evening, when neighbors and family had gathered in the garden fearful of another quake, or maybe a building collapse, Mama whispered the *fatiha* repeatedly under her breath. The entire neighborhood seemed to be there, taking refuge in the open space. They echoed like a chorus. *Nothing is built like this anymore.* Would their buildings survive? They fretted. Aunty had arrived with a black suitcase that held her jewels. She was the kind of person who was probably more worried about the banks, if they would open again. Her brow remained furrowed the entire evening, and she didn't say a word. By nightfall the radio announced that the last of the tremors had been felt, and it was *probably* safe to *assume* that any building still upright was *probably relatively* safe to return to. We went upstairs. Eventually the garden emptied out. Mama spent that night praying, on the armchair by her bedroom window, going to bed only when the sun rose.

One day passes, then another, and nothing has happened, so H's father says maybe now it was safe to go. Wednesday, midday showing? I nod, as if she can see. Let's take the metro? I hear her father responding before I do. He screams. Have you lost your mind? I don't plan on telling Mama, she will worry and sense my worry too. I don't know if I'm afraid of death, but I am not keen on being blown up. H believes everything is connected, the stars, the moon, our lives, particles, air, the sea. No matter what you do, you are already figured into a larger program of the universe. Whether she takes the metro or not, if she is meant to be blown up by a bomb, it will happen, one way or another. It will catch up with her, possibly within minutes. It is just a matter of time for scientists to name the theorem. Her conviction intrigues me. In astronomy class the professor had raised one eyebrow as she delivered her hypothesis. He was American, the only American, and asked if she had been watching *The Simpsons*? *The Simpsons*? None of us knew what that was. Yet H still listened to her father, a retired mathematician, who calculated probability for everything. Chances of being blow up. Breaking your leg. Getting an A. Getting married. Getting divorced. Having a car accident. Winning the lottery. *Baba coming back?* When I asked her *why* she listened to anyone at all if *everything* was already predetermined, she shrugged and said it was all programmed, *even* the listening to her father. *And* the rescheduling of our cinema plans. Really? What about provoking fate? I get a piercing look. The reports of men throwing acid on women for being indiscreet are exaggerated. She hopes I don't believe the hype. I do. But what is *indiscreet* anyway? Wearing short sleeves? Open necklines? Going naked? We all ask this. When had there become such a thing, *indiscreet*? I decide that H is the happiest, most well-adjusted person I know. I will start my film with her, asking if she is angry.

I sit on the sofa opposite Mama. She asks how my day was. Okay. Yours? They caught two terrorists on the road to Sinai. Mama knows I am asking about her day. When she answers about the news, I take it to mean the day was hard. Some afternoons I come home and find the door to Baba's office ajar. Mama will be sitting on his chair, staring, into nothing. She had stopped asking the lady to clean it months before I realized, and now I could see the dust even through the slight crack of the door, illuminated by rays of sunlight streaming through the wooden shutters. Mama talked more and more about the news. Again she worried about us and Iran. It was no longer about the veil. It didn't scare anyone, since almost everyone seemed to be wearing it and no one had really changed. A study that plays repeatedly on TV claims eighty percent of veiled women wear it for economic reasons. It means they don't have to do their hair or buy fancy clothes. It is cheaper to be veiled. The other twenty percent wear it for other reasons. They don't say what percentage wear it because of religion. It is the terrorists who scare Mama and everyone else now. The only person who doesn't seem to have fears is Grandmama, not of death or disease or bombs. She says what happens will. I should enjoy every moment I have. I listen intently, wishing Mama worried less too. I look at her, sitting across from me in her spot on the sofa in her robe, thinner than she used to be. I wonder about her thoughts.

We are watching Channel One. They are playing a montage of images to the sounds of Verdi's *Aida*. They play it often. Every day and now several times a day. I know it well. 1954. Alexandria. Nasser's speech. The withdrawal of the British from Egypt. Cut. Headshot. The Muslim Brotherhood member who tried to assassinate him that day. He fired eight shots, which missed. Nasser didn't so much as flinch. He just kept speaking. *Let them kill me* he said. *If Gamal Abdel Nasser should die, each of you shall be Gamal Abdel Nasser. If Gamal Abdel Nasser should die, each of you shall be Gamal Abdel Nasser. If Gamal Abdel Nasser should die, each of you shall be Gamal Abdel Nasser If Gamal Abdel Nasser should die, each of you shall be Gamal Abdel Nasser.* We are made to write out these words in an exam. After the picture of the attempted killer, they show many of Nasser. In his motorcade. Standing in a convertible waving to the crowds. Leaning forward. Streets lined with millions waving back. The crescendo of the third act of *Aida*. As I walk in the streets downtown, this montage bookending every other program, I can see people watching, entranced. I begin to realize the power of these montages, these visual narratives of my childhood. We had all seen these scenes innumerable times. Images imprinted in us through repetition. I wonder how to use this in my film. Even the background music, playing as if from memory. I stare at Mama, then turn my head back to the TV. They have moved to Sadat and footage of the October 6 parade, followed by the only image of his wounded and limp body that had ever been seen. Then his wife, children, grandchildren, the international dignitaries at his funeral. They spend extra seconds on photos of Nixon, Ford, Carter. After that come mug shots of the killers. Dark pictures, possibly photocopied, to make faces more blackened, more haunting. To this day I don't recognize Baba's cousin, even though I know him by name. His sister is always at Grandmama's. We call her the Bulldozer, because of her size. She knows this and laughs one day that at least she isn't the Terrorist like her brother. I want to ask her how she felt about him, how they had turned out so differently after spending the first eleven, twelve, maybe thirteen years of their lives side by side. Did she feel love for him? Did she have any sense who he would become? I wonder, but it isn't the kind of thing one is to talk about. I raise it with H instead. She tells me that if *she* had a brother who killed, she would let him be. Fate and the universe would take revenge. But she would give him the silent treatment. Love him inside but blank him, pretend he wasn't even in the room, *even* if he spoke to her. She delivers this with absolute certainty, as if it's something she has already thought through at length. I wonder what Baba might have done if this were his brother and not his cousin. Baba always used to say that as we age, things change, we become more rigid, and then eventually, most of us, become forgiving again. He called it the cycle of life. Much he had said had been true, the things I remembered anyway. The things he told me. There was much I didn't know, and many things I imagine I had inherited, borrowed, maybe even imposed on him, the man I wanted him to be, pieced together, fading memories held tight by strands.

Mama and I sit watching TV until the call to prayer. It sounds from the mosque across the river and echoes into the house. The president had issued a decree banning mosque speakers above a certain decibel, but they had become louder again after a few months of quieting down. It's the most pertinent daily reminder of the increasing antagonism between the Brotherhood and the state. Mama prays but shakes her head every time the muezzin begins to warm his voice into the loudspeaker. Her neck tenses and she shuts her eyes for a moment. She said that God had helped her in the years since Baba left, but it didn't mean religion had to be imposed like this. They didn't have to force it all down our throats.

When the massacre had happened, even Amina

the housekeeper said she was against this new Islam. She had missed work that day and come on Saturday instead. Mama was still asleep when the doorbell rang. I stuck my head out of the window. Who? She waved and called her name. Mama is sleeping. I can wait. Do you want to leave her a message? I'm coming to work. Today is your day? I didn't come on Wednesday because of the accident. I buzzed her in. The back steps are narrow. She clasped one side of her galabia in one hand and put her other on the black metal banister. She heaved herself up onto the first step. Paused, and looked up at me. She was already out of breath. I know that she walks twenty minutes to the bus stop from her house. Takes one bus then another. The second drops her off five minutes away. It takes her twenty more minutes to walk those five minutes. She lives in a shed on the roof of a building with a single lightbulb and no running water. I looked at her with a pained expression on my face. I didn't want to watch her climb the two flights but also felt I should. Can I help? God bless you. I moved my head in awkward acknowledgment. Took half a step back. Watched as she labored her way up.

Amina changed out of her galabia, shielded by the door of the broom closet. I sat in the kitchen. She asked when Mama woke. I shrugged. Maybe an hour?

She went to the fridge. Opened it, peered inside. Amina knew she could have whatever she wanted. She took out four eggs. Maneuvered them into one hand. Opened the drawer of the fridge with the other. Took out two *baladi* breads. Nudged the fridge door closed with her voluminous hip. She paid no notice to me as she went to the stove. Put the eggs down on the counter. Barricaded them with the bread. Oil. Salt. Pepper. Cracked the eggs into the pan and let them fry on the highest heat, the oil splattering everywhere. Turned the left burner on and put the bread on the flames. As she was flipping it over with her fingers, Mama walked in. It was early for her. She had slept badly. She was wearing her red satin robe, one Baba had brought back from a trip. She asked how we were as she went to the counter. Unplugged the kettle. Took it to the sink. Filled it with water. With her back to Amina, she asked how she was. *So you didn't come on Wednesday?* Mama had started to ask questions like this. Questions that were weighted. Questions that had already been answered. Questions that pretended to pose themselves but were rather statements, usually of disapproval. She said them with her neck tensed and slightly shaking. Amina turned off the stove and told Mama that she would never believe what she had been through. They had surrounded her whole neighborhood and every single building, armed, masked special 777 forces and tanks. Weapons like we have never seen before.

The massacre had taken place in the early morning on the eastern bank of Luxor, just before Hatshepsut's Temple. The cruise ship had been approaching the city when the gunmen opened fire. Forty-five minutes of continuous rounds. Sixty-two people killed. Dozens injured. Within minutes of the attack, the message circulated Cairo's state security headquarters. Special forces were dispatched to all the Islamist strongholds. Amina's neighborhood, across the river from our island, was the first place sealed shut. We heard sirens that morning but didn't know what they were. The neighborhood was nicknamed the Islamic Republic. Kandahar. I had never been but could see it from my bedroom window, the beginning of it, right across the river. It extended for miles. Amina said they had been stuck in their room for two days until they cleared them. It was Al-Gamaa Al-Islaamiya, she said. Not the Brotherhood. Mama looked with brows raised and asked what the difference was. This was another of those shrouded statements. Amina put her hands to her hips. Of course there is a difference, a vast one. The Brotherhood doesn't believe in violence. Mama tilted her head sideways and looked at her sternly. Amina was quick to blurt, *Not all of them. I swear Sayed had nothing to do with this. Many of the Brotherhood are denouncing violence, they are beginning to, the groups are different now, separate.* Mama had never trusted the husband. He had come to the house when Amina was sick to collect her salary. He had a wild beard and glum face. Carried a short stick. Didn't look women in the eye. Wouldn't shake hands. Mama had warned Amina she had to be careful what she was dragged into, but Amina insisted she had nothing to do with any of his business. After the bombings began, she said that even her husband was having second thoughts about the Brotherhood, even the nonviolent faction of them. He was thinking of leaving them altogether. Many of their members had left. Mama told her that she had to realize that I went to university right near the site of the last bomb. Even though it was aimed at tourists, it might easily have hit me. Amina shook her head and asked *God the Greatest* to erase and forgive these words. Allah protect the girl. Mama poured the hot water into her mug. She seemed on the verge of an emotion I had never seen from her before. *Anger?* I imagined this as a scene in my film and picked up a Biro from the table, making a note on the back of my hand. I watched as Amina tore a strip of bread and dipped it into the pan, scooped out a piece of fried egg, then circled the bread in the oil. She stuffed her mouth and chewed. Mama took a sip of her coffee and shook her head.

I go into my bedroom and sit at my desk. It's facing the big window overlooking the Nile. I can't see the Nile. I can't see anything except the overgrown mango trees. We keep talking about pruning them. The gardener says nobody in the country knows how to prune. He doesn't know what we mean. He tells us he can cut them down if that's what we want. Mama gets upset when he says this. She slams the window. Shakes her head. We let the trees grow. They are higher than the house. But there aren't any mangoes. There haven't been mangoes in five, six, maybe seven years. Every summer I wait to see. Maybe this year they will fruit again. And then they don't. I ask the gardener and he says the soil is bad. How does the soil become bad? He shrugs his shoulders. It's just the way it is, something from Allah. I think of maybe starting my film with the mango trees. I flip through my script and wonder about the soil.

I start writing:

Over lunch Dido says the only way our lives will change is if we demand it. People like our cousin in

America are the reason we're in stagnation. Leaving is the greatest evil. Then silence. Or maybe the other way around. He isn't sure. We just can't be passive, he knows that. My friend's theory is nonsense. Nothing is pre-planned. Every moment is pregnant with the possibility for change. It's important to look at everything that happens with a view for the future. Dido is eating the eggs that Mama has made. They are covered in Tabasco. He is wearing jeans and a casual shirt but also a tie. It's flung back over his shoulder. His work doesn't require him to wear a tie but he likes to. It's a sign of respect for the cases he's working on. He chews slowly and speaks between bites.

I make notes in the margin: Have we inherited defeat, the very spirit of it? Is it seeped into who we are? Do we have to reconcile with our parents' losses to build again? Where does Dido's anger figure in? *If in fact we are angry.* I circle this and think about all that I feel has been stolen from me, from us. I wonder if *anger* is too simple a word, too reductive. Maybe I could have a conversation or debate between Uncle and Dido about this? I underline and write out the word *languor.* I don't want my film to be scripted, but I have a sense of what I would like the tenor, atmosphere, of it to be. I want to create enough cues and structure for it to be a cinematic feature, and enough space to also include spontaneity and cinéma vérité. I write: *Quotidian.* I wonder what it would mean to have people from my life acting scenes as well as trailed with a camera every day. Could I script certain events? Or have someone recount them as part of a family discussion? Like showing the different viewpoints that reflected the complexity of the national psyche, exposed in the days after Mubarak returned from Addis. *Maybe something that captures the gap of generations?* For days afterwards the TV played, almost on loop, Mubarak giving his speech on landing back at Cairo International Airport. *Suddenly I found a blue van blocking the road, and somebody jumped to the ground. A machine gun started. . . . I realized there were bullets coming at our car. I saw those who shot at me.* Everyone said it was the Israelis. Guests on Channel One and Two all said *el yahoud.* The Jews. Mossad. There were Ethiopian Jews too, they told us. I thought Kebbe might have been one. Nobody asked, but it was presumed. Mama and Baba had never minded the Jews. They had many Jewish friends and loved Kebbe. It was the Israelis they had a problem with. People had started putting up posters on their buildings wishing the president a speedy recovery. They made posters with the Star of David washed over with dripping red paint. The Jews had blood on their hands. Everyone said this. People worried it would be '67 all over again. Then one day, a few days later, new evidence was found. The gunmen were Arab. Uncle was with us that day. We heard the news on TV as it broke. He erupted, about there being no difference between us. Mama and I both looked at him, eyes wide. Spit flew from his mouth to the floor. He meant the Arabs and Jews. Under his breath he muttered that common sense is not that common. I could see Mama's neck tense. I didn't know if it was something Uncle was saying or his spit. I sat there until he stopped talking and we were all quiet. I asked if anyone wanted a glass of water. Uncle asked me how my writing was going.

I gazed at Uncle and Mama that day and wondered about fate. Could I build all this into what I'm writing, my script, the eventual film? I want to do something different, merge forms, speak to people on the street about their desires, and also capture this internal life, the intimate moments at home, the mundane. How did we land in our lives? The silence and the evenings in front of the TV are as comforting as they are fraught. In my mind's eye I envisage Baba, his absence ever present in the questions unasked. Even Dido and I don't talk about it, though we talk about everything else. I imagine the questions linger for everyone. There had been problems with the government. They were selective about who they went after. It is all I know. It might be all anyone knows, even Baba himself. In ways I understand what Dido means when he says it should be the source of my anger, that my placid exterior is a mask. An arbitrary system is an unjust system, he says. Or maybe it's no system at all. Maybe H can play the main protagonist, enacting parts and playing herself in others. Maybe she's right that I should just write a book.

Mama has her hands crossed on her chest. She sits upright, as if watching and listening intently. An advertisement for Al Jawhara tea. Three men sit at a café playing backgammon. Two wear safari suits. One is in a gold-threaded galabia. Colored tea lights are strung across an alley. As they play, they begin to slouch into their chairs. One man nods off into sleep. Enter the belly dancer. Singing, dancing, a tray of glasses with tea balanced on her hand. Her body writhes. The café is suddenly packed with people. The men perk up. They dance around her. Uncle's face is blank.

PART THREE

SUMMER 2014, CAIRO

THE CLEANING LADY FOUND Uncle in bed one morning a few months before the revolution. His coffee was untouched. Biscuit crumbs were on his bedcover. He was sitting upright, holding the newspaper, not moving. They said it was a heart attack, high blood pressure. The last time I had seen him was on the Sunday after they pulled down the church. He came with three newspapers and rang the bell insistently. I stuck my head out of the window ready to shout. Young boys were always ringing our bell and running away. I saw Uncle's bald head and went down to greet him. We went up the back stairs together. He put one hand on the banister and hauled himself up. I could hear his breath getting heavier ahead of me. He asked if Mama was home. Mama was always home in the mornings. Some days she wouldn't come out of her bedroom until noon. Uncle paused at the first floor and peered in. Each time he came, he would say that he hadn't been downstairs since Granny died. I would tell him to come, look. He would shake his head, pat my shoulder, look up at the stairs ahead of him, and tell me that it was better this way. Some memories need to be preserved. He didn't want to write over them with something new.

I was living downstairs by then. I slept in the room where Granny and Nesma had lived and died. Their things were in storage in the basement, except for Granny's bed, which was now in Mama's room, the same room she was born in. We went up to Mama's floor. I put my key in the door and coerced it until the lock turned. All the locks in the house had problems. Some of them opened backwards, others jammed. Mama refused to change them. She worried the locksmith would change the lock and keep a copy of the keys for himself. I had become skeptical like her. Everyone would cheat you. Uncle would say that corruption and thievery were what made the country. Without those things it would fall apart. A low-lying level of corruption was critical, something like oil on a machine. Dido and he argued about this endlessly.

Dido had paced the room the last time it came up, not long before Uncle died. He was adamant. He didn't participate in this *insidious* corruption. Anarchy was better. Uncle asked him. Did he tip the parking attendant? The man who helped with his papers at the Mugamma? Dido gestured with his shoulders and hands as if to say, *Ridiculous question.* Uncle laughed. Dido barked back that it was culture not corruption. He was part of a movement that would take to the streets chanting about being fed up with the status quo. *Kifaya,* it's enough. He had tried repeatedly to get me to go with him to the marches, to make a film called *Kifaya.* I promised I would go one day, but just not *that* day. Every few weeks he would try again, but I knew that deep down he knew. Activism was in the genes, and if not, it came from upbringing. We are informed by the experiences and behaviors of those around us. Dido loved me, but when he said these things, I could feel his disappointment. I knew I lacked the gene. I was more interested in abstracting experience with my writing and films than representing it. Unless it was the mundane, like a nine-minute short I filmed in a record store downtown. The owner was weary at first. He asked who I was making a film for. Why was I making a film? Who would see it? What would I do with it? Why his shop? He said I could film, then changed his mind. I showed him other films I had made. I went to him again. Again. We drank tea. Eventually he agreed. I filmed. Hours of B roll. A customer comes in with a CD he has bought of Umm Kulthum. He tells the shop owner to go to the second song. He asks him to listen. The song is one hour and forty-four minutes long. It happens in minute twenty-three. The quality isn't what it should be. He knows Umm Kulthum, and her voice doesn't crack like it does here. They listen. She is singing at a decibel higher than she should. It lasts a second, maybe it's intentional? It's a crack, she lost control. But she never lost control. Is it age? Was it? It's just a bad recording? It is a bad recording. It must be. They call a man walking by from off the street. What does he think? The café owner next door. The *bawab* of a building across the alley. Does her voice crack? This is her most famous concert, it can't be. They play minute twenty-three over and over. They turn to me and ask what I think. In my mind I think that I can just sit there for hours, camera on, listening like them. This was what Dido had meant about placid, I thought.

Uncle had walked into the house and collapsed onto the sofa. He asked me for a glass of water or something fizzy. There was no sign of Mama. He put his neck back and tried to catch his breath. I could tell his heaving was as much about the church as his weight. The police had gone into a village on the outskirts of Cairo and bulldozed a church to the ground overnight. It lacked a permit, they said. In the newspaper there were pictures of Copts protesting, crying, wailing around the rubble. There were also pictures of young men, *kūfiyyahs* wrapped around their mouths and noses, dust clouding their knees down, arms hurled backwards, or forward, rocks flying through the air. Their faces strained. A friend, a longtime newspaper editor, told me he had never seen anything like it before. In all my years, and I am sixty-one, he said. The youth looked like they were in Gaza. It was the same kind of despair. I told Uncle when he came. I knew he would look and understand. He had been saying all year that it was untenable. *La faim.* He told me to watch for certain things. The price of tomatoes and okra. If the man carrying the bread on his head as he cycles is whistling or not. If people are watching TV at cafés, or sitting in silence, or debating. If the radio begins to play repeated patriotic songs. Without tomatoes and okra we can't live, he said. I didn't like okra but understood. It was prickly on the outside and like slime inside. Deceptive. People consumed it almost daily, scooping it into bread and gulping it down, oblivious to texture. It was the cheapest vegetable. We cooked tomatoes with everything. Every day the opposition newspapers would print a picture of a cart piled high with tomatoes. The price per kilo was hand-drawn on a card in their midst. That summer I set up a camera on a downtown corner each morning and zoomed in from across the street. Carts piled like pyramids. The better tomatoes on top, the bad ones hidden beneath. One minute, three minutes, five. If nobody bothered me, I would have let the camera roll all day. Invariably I was asked to leave. When I asked one cart owner why, he said we all know that tomatoes are politics, he didn't want any trouble. The prime minister had announced he couldn't do anything more about the price of tomatoes. He had done everything he could. He also couldn't do anything about the power cuts and heat, except change the clocks, to put Cairo into a different time zone, on GMT+3. It happened arbitrarily one day. Two days later I found out, when I was late to meet a friend. For others it took a week. Mama had stopped buying tomatoes. She said they were exorbitant and we could do without. I reached for a glass from the cabinet. I poured water from the bottle Mama must have taken out of the freezer at some point in the night. Nobody drank tap water anymore, the government had announced some years ago that it was contaminated, and the fridge was so old it hardly cooled. We would fill the freezer with plastic bottles of water, then take them out and let them sit on the counter and melt through the day.

Uncle and Mama argued that morning. He insisted the demolition proved the government had been behind an attack on a Coptic village that had gone uninvestigated by the state. Mama was adamant it couldn't be. Her best friend Farida was a Copt and said the government was the only thing protecting them. Mubarak and the Pope were one. It was politics, pure and simple. Uncle turned to me and asked what I thought. All through the summer he had been saying we were on the brink. He told me I should be filming everything, and keeping notes, a detailed journal. I had to learn to feel the air change. It was all in the sounds, the way particles moved, echoed. The sounds of the city had shifted. We had sat on the balcony on consecutive Sundays over the entire summer and listened. He pointed to the reverberations of car horns. How the honking had both quieted and intensified, taken on a different impatience. We listened to the voices that echoed in from the streets and across the river. The constant chatter had given way to more abrupt bursts of expression. Something was pacified, followed by discharge. We could make out none of it,

but the very tenor had shifted. We also listened for
when the sound of the city suddenly stopped. A/Cs
and the drone of business and machines and genera-
tors would roar and then collapse. For a moment there
would be quiet, then the cars and the honking and a
rumble would begin. It was a sign of excess, a city over
capacity. We were breaking down. It was like a building, Uncle said. Filled beyond measurable proportions, badly wired, with extensions, borrowed power,
borrowed pipes. He would look at me and shake his
head, say nothing, but I knew what he was thinking.
He had said it many times before over the years. This
was what my generation was inheriting. It was up to
us to mitigate the losses, the mistakes. Uncle tried to
hold on to as many of the better memories as he could,
many with Granny and Mama on this same balcony,
eating mangoes, watermelon, white cheese, watching
the Nile and looking out onto the expanse of green
fields. It reached the horizon, and seemed to extend
further, into the unknown. All we could see now beyond the sliver of Nile and the bushes of the garden
were miles of a sepia city, and past that, in a horizon
marked by a chalk line of rust red, the informal settlements. They made me think back to when Baba used
to take me with him to the factory when I was a child.
Back then the roads in the center of town were paved,

but once you got to the outskirts of the city, much of it was dirt track. You knew you had come to the city's end, it was like reaching the edge of the earth, where one line and color and atmosphere ended, and a plunge into something less certain began. Baba would slow as he maneuvered the car down from the tarmac onto the rougher, pebbled tracks. The sprawling tapestry of sepia and unfinished redbrick blocks that now extends for miles was then just desert, or crops. The colors around us changed. As I looked out from the balcony, I remembered all this. Rows and rows of redbrick and concrete buildings, unfinished, not connected in any way to the infrastructure of the built city. It was there, Dido had said, that the fight would erupt. He urged me to read *Vertigo*. Set in 2030, it was prophetic. Dido spoke of the fight as if he wanted a war, but he was a romantic, and I knew that in his heart what he really wanted was for comrades, dissidents, to unite, raise a flag, occupy the streets, and talk about love, peace, revolution. I couldn't imagine it, but I listened, read Ginsberg and Darwish to him aloud, asked him to describe what came after this utopia he envisioned. What would he do next?

That summer, sitting on the terrace with Uncle, I asked him what he thought. Is it possible? Could it happen? What would it mean? Uncle said it was inevitable, eventually some change would come, but much more so he wished our lives were different. To fall in love, to build a life with a loved one, was the greatest freedom. He hoped I, we, would have that one day. He understood that none of it was so straightforward. Most young people can't afford to build independent lives. Love is a calculation of resources and pedigree. Uncle never spoke about his own love, but I knew of her. They met in college, but she had been married by arrangement to a family friend in their sophomore year. Uncle promised he would wait for her until the day she divorced. They wrote letters to each other, mailed from across the city, looking out at the same horizon, the same skyline. They would meet when they could, at the supermarket, the club, on the corner of the street before she picked up her children from school. Dido had told me that Uncle would wait for her forever. Her husband would never leave her. It was a matter of pride. It was one of the things Dido encouraged me to fight for, that *we* had to fight for, the right to divorce as women. Uncle died waiting. He died before her. We had never spoken about his own emotions, but he was the only one who talked to me about desires. I had found the courage to ask him about our cousin in America that summer. What happened? Why had he left? Why would no one talk about it? Why did Mama's neck tense whenever his name came up? What were the *problems*? Why couldn't he come back? Uncle had looked me straight in the eye and said that I must have known. *I have a sense.* He paused. Muttered something about the terror of the state, then paused again. They caught him in a car with a boy. You know how it is, he said. I couldn't understand if they didn't see it in others or it was something they just chose to ignore. I turned my eyes down to the newspaper and asked him if he was hungry.

Mama appeared through the *mashrabiyya* doors in her robe. She had heard us talking. Did she want a coffee? She shook her head as she tied a second bow on her satin sash. Her robe was a pale pistachio. She had stopped wearing the one Baba had given her the autumn before. I had sat in her bedroom as she went through closets, bringing out winter clothes, packing away summer ones. On the armchair in her room she made a pile of things to give away. It was the first time I had seen Mama give away anything. I lay on her bed, elbow propped, head on my hand, her back towards me as she rummaged. I could see my reflection in her mirrored closet doors, and as well her face. That was the day she told me about the dream. The house had been painted white, there was a white wooden fence around it, the garden was in full bloom. She saw Granny. Flowers sprouted everywhere. Flowers that had never grown before. Tulips. Colors we'd never seen. The grass shimmered emerald. It was pouring with rain. A cherry-covered cake was placed on the lawn. The rain fell around it. The dream was a good one. The white was an indication of new beginnings, and the rain a good omen. I asked why Granny was there, what she thought it meant. Mama raised her eyebrows as if to say who knows, then said that only God knew.

I got up and went through her pile of clothes to give away. I wanted to ask if she was sure about the robe, and what about the white silk blouse, and this belt, really? They were all things Baba had bought. I swallowed the thought as I felt it rise and roll onto my tongue. I had cleared out downstairs myself two summers earlier with a tepid urgency, getting rid of what I could from the past. Mama had come down as I was putting things in bags, going through drawers, marking piles for storage or to be thrown away. I had felt her in the main room before I saw her, the tension of her body emanating. I could tell she was uncomfortable. Downstairs had been closed for years.

Nobody spoke about it anymore. It was as if the floor, its entire lifetime, had been banished or erased. Then Granny and Nesma visited me in my dreams, calling me downstairs. I saw them in the dream, standing on the stairs, repeating my name, telling me to join them. I wondered if it was about death. They say you know in the days before you die that they're your final ones, signs come to you. Or was it just a dream about space, my own consciousness of it? When I told Mama, she had been sitting at her dressing table combing her hair. I could see her inhale deeply, her chest rising, her neck pushing back against her head, but she didn't say a word. Her pause was so long, it felt like disapproval, and I got up after a while and left. Then the dream came again. That August, finally, Mama told me I could do as I pleased. She said it without words, just with her eyes and a nudge of head. Ours wasn't a culture used to change. Permanancy was valued. We lived in the same places we were born in. We married and moved around the corner. A job was held for decades. The less change, the less movement, the better. It was a view to stability rather than the oppression I had internalized it to be. Everyone we knew preserved lives as they were, over generations. Sofas stayed covered in plastic, glass cabinets with proliferating displays not to be touched, every gift, every token, every ticket, stuffed somewhere, or in a drawer. Most people's homes were like time capsules, offering panoramic views of every year until the present one. The narrative of Granny's floor had begun in 1940 and ended three days after she died, in 1983. The piles of hoarded newspapers and magazines spanned those years. The gadgets, gifts, flyers, phone books, postcards. Her letters were stored in shoe boxes and tied with ribbon. The last one, dated December 31, 1981. It was postmarked Lalibela. Inside was a string of brass beads. It was signed *Devotedly yours*. The letter before that was locally stamped, from the brother of Sadat, offering greetings for the Eid. A few days before came a government notice about tax. Mama had asked me to keep certain things, even though she knew we might never look at them again and until that moment we had no sense they had even existed. I put what I could in boxes, covered the furniture in sheets, bubble-wrapped paintings, glasswear, porcelain, china, and silver. Boxes and boxes of letters, postcards, photographs, film reels, negatives, crochet thread, stamps, brooches. Suitcases of clothes, Granny's, folded and put away. Everything was moved to the basement. I kept a single photograph from Granny's collection, framed it, and had it hung on a wall by the entrance. It is of downstairs, one day when Granny was still alive.

It looks like it might be winter, judging from dress, although the house is always cold. Granny is sitting in a corner, Nesma by her feet, both of them drowned out by the deep cocoa tones of the furniture and curtains and paintings and the great grandfather clock looming nearby. A blanket covers Granny's lap. A furry shawl is flung over Nesma's shoulders. A seven-layered chandelier cuts across one side of the frame. Granny's lips are a deep pink, jumping out amid somber tones. I kept that, and as well a series of Granny's paintings; miniature, Polaroid-size oils of the view from the main terrace, painted on November 28 of each year since the house was built. They hung on the largest wall in the sitting room, off-center, to the right. The palette changed very slightly on each canvas, from greens and earth tones to scales, eventually, of sepia, rust, and grays. Four of the years were missing. Mama didn't know why. The gaps of those years were left as spaces on the wall that themselves had become tinted with time. It was the single wall I didn't paint white. Once I moved downstairs Mama would come down often and look at the paintings. She would sit with her coffee cup on the rocking chair facing them and tell me that it was like watching a film. The stories would come flooding back, filling her, occupying her mind's eye.

The last morning with Uncle, Mama had walked into the living room and stared at the newspapers. At the bottom of the front page was a picture of Toshka, the president's New Valley Project, intended to turn thousands of acres of desert into agricultural land. Uncle called it the greatest failed promise of any president. Nasser's project had been the Aswan High Dam. Sadat's the Suez Canal. Mubarak's was Toshka. Every day *Al-Ahram* ran stories about the promise of Toshka. It had been ten years. Mama had looked at the picture, the desert landscape with strata of color, and let her eyes drift, then asked Uncle, seemingly out of nowhere, about the paintings downstairs. He tilted his head sideways and asked if she remembered the day they sat on the balcony eating mangoes until they both got sick? It was the day after Granny had painted the eighteenth miniature in the series. She had propped it up against the ledge of the balcony. It had always been his favorite, because it was like the horizon, the beginning of a palette shift. I made a mental note to look at that painting later. *Maybe it could even be the cover of my book*. Then I pushed myself up from the sofa and stood over Uncle and Mama. I have to go. Where? *Dar Merit*. Why? I'm editing a manuscript for a forthcoming book. The first-ever translation of Khairallah C. Ali.. A novel? A story of listlessness, and falling in love on the coast. A love story that is understood later, long after its moments of conception. Mama slowly nodded her head. Uncle told me I should pay more attention to my own writing. He was still waiting for my book. I smiled, told him I was working on it, leaned over, kissed him on one cheek, taking steps backwards and giving Mama a half wave with my lowered hand. She told me to be careful. Uncle told her to let me be and kept talking. I heard him tell Mama that my writing would free me, and then after some murmuring I couldn't make out, he repeated the word catastrophe, *ma'saa,* as I went down the steps. He may have been speaking about Toshka, or even the Copts. It never occurred to me that he might have been referring to me. I had no sense it would be our final goodbye. Later I wondered if Mama might have known, if that's why she had asked about the paintings. She had premonitions about things.

I walked around the house that day and saw a neighbor from afar. She was one of the ones who lived with her shutters closed. I hadn't seen her in months. She looked shrunken and sallow. Her daughter, an only child, had fallen out of the window of her fifth-floor bedroom eight months earlier. The parking attendant had found her at dawn. She was Dido's age. He had known her through a friend. When Mama had called to offer condolences, they told her it was a sugar coma. Diabetes. She had been sitting at the window and fell out. Dido said it was more than that. She had been depressed for years. I watched the mother, hunched over the walking stick she now used, Mama's age but looking eighty. I avoided her, my eyes down, tracing the potholed street. At the corner, the *bawab* of the next-door building was watching TV. It was set up on the pavement, and he sat on a small wooden stool. I traced his wire, up to a balcony on the first floor. He heard me pass, raised his head, nodded, smiled. I could hear the laughter of Ismail Yaseen from his set, then Sabah's voice break into song. I raised my arm, trying to stop a taxi. The black and white cars slowed as they approached. *Downtown*, I shouted. Most of them sped off as quickly as they had slowed beside me, sometimes shaking their heads in apology, other times as if to say, Are you crazy? Downtown was impossible to move through by car. There were barricades everywhere, around all the government buildings, streets had been blocked, traffic rerouted. There was no explanation as to why. It happened overnight. People said it was out of fear, but fear of what, we didn't know. On one street they said it was because the president's son had bought property there. They hadn't closed the street but rather redirected traffic to go from north to south, instead of the other way. There was no logic as to why. One taxi driver tells me I'm better off walking. I wait fifteen more minutes, as each taxi slows and zooms off. One hesitates, asks how much I will pay, hesitates some more, then declines apologetically. Nobody walks, but that day I did. I walked down the corniche, along the Nile, under sagging trees, over broken pavements, piles of garbage, past the cultural center that had been started in an abscess of space under the bridge. I walked all the way down the fenced-off Nile. I could see none of the river except at the rowing club where a metal gate was flung open. Hedges had overgrown and turned ashen and been littered and then covered with corrugated metal. Walls had been made higher. There was no sense, anymore, of being surrounded by waters. It was another reminder of the battle over the Nile's waters. Before he died, Uncle had said that he hoped Ethiopia would submit. He would turn his head up and say it as if making a wish, throwing it out into the sky to be heard or maybe caught in the wind and blown to open ears. Uncle said our future, *possibility,* was all in the Nile waters. The dam could never be built. It would be colonialism all over again.

· · ·

It has been almost four years since Uncle died. Forty-one months since the revolution. Like all my friends I find it hard to sleep through the night. My sleep is fitful. I get up, I pace, I check the news, Twitter, I try to work. My desk faces a wall. A sketch of Mama's, a portrait, hangs above it. Piles surround me. Newspapers, books. On the floor, leaned against walls, opened randomly, left on the sofa. What I once thought would be a script is slowly being turned into a book. It's an hour past dawn, but the heat is already scorching. My shutters are partially down, blocking out the sun. A plastic fan whines in the corner. In the background I can hear the chatter of birds. I pick up Mahmoud Darwish's *Memory of Forgetfulness*, Booklet No. 48, fiction, Nawal El Saadawi writing for the art biennial Documenta. I browse, leaf through pages, book after book, mindlessly, searching. I flip through a photocopy of an Arabic study on the literature of defeat, what was conceived in the aftermath of '67. It is described by one writer cited as *a new language that spoke to the times.* Everything was stripped down to fundamentals, bare, deflated. I read about this new language, one I have read through its novels for years. *The more ornate social realism of such prominent writers as Naguib Mahfouz and the virtuous eloquence of Arabic literature were abandoned for more experimental, fragmented works that expressed the anxieties and crises at hand.* I pick up another book. Another. Everything has resonance. I wonder about structure, and form. Genre. Can literature, the novel, be written in the form of a script? At what point would it become that, *a script*? I think about this as I relive summers and try to write, grapple with the beginnings of a manuscript. The summer before Uncle died. The things that were said. The summer before things changed. Dido and I becoming estranged.

We fought sitting at a café on a pedestrian street in *El Borsa* downtown. Dido was smoking apple-flavored *shisha*, I was drinking mint tea served extra sweet. Over the years our views had differed and veered apart. Dido believed fervently that anarchy was better than the despotism we had. My reservations were inherited. He had hoped I might turn out as political as him, but I'd failed him in every way. He consumed literature voraciously, but thought writing in a country like ours to be an exercise in passivity, a luxurious musing, not a tool for change. He spoke of the need for an urgency to one's actions, a physicality. I insisted writing is an action, becomes a physicality. We debated this often, argued about it, sometimes even wrote impassioned letters that we would read to each other out loud. When we fought, though, it was about the two young men who sauntered off the street and sat at a table down from ours. They held hands and wore tight T-shirts. One of them had a yellow headband through his hair. We sat in silence for a long time, Dido inhaling his pipe, watching them from an angle, his head slightly revealing of his scrutiny. I watched with no attempt to conceal my gaze. People walked by. Young men sat down. Two girls with wild curls. Four young boys, also in tight T-shirts, also holding hands. They put two tables together and asked for the unused chairs from nearby. Dido and I looked on. I could hear him inhale. As he released, blowing a single smoke ring into the air, I watched him raise two fingers languidly, gesturing with them and as well with his eyes. His charcoal was out. He wanted a refill. We looked past the white robes of the man placing more cubes of lit charcoal into the mouth of the *shisha*. We looked past the growing crowd around us and to the table with the two young men. A man in a gray safari shirt and faded black trousers had walked towards them. He had been standing at the corner for close to an hour. I had noticed his shoes. Dido had too. They were familiar shoes. Shoes we saw a lot. Shoes of the undercover police. They were pointed, with a ledge. With his head the man gestured to the extra plastic chair at the table. Could he join? The young men hovered forward from their waists, their feet verging on pushing themselves up from the ground. Their gesture: *of course*. He pulled back the chair and sat. The server rushing forward, saluting him, bowing. The young men in their tight T-shirts, touching hands, leaned forward. Words were exchanged. Dido flicked his head, so fiercely that the tube of his *shisha* leaped from his hand onto the floor. He swore under his breath. Minutes passed. The man and his shoes got up and walked away. The young men resumed their laughter. Dido fumed. I could see it in his nostrils, in the movement of his chest. He tapped his foot nervously. His thigh trembled. We shared a friend who had fled the country years before. He had been on the moored Queen Boat-turned-nightclub when it was raided by plainclothes state security agents. Someone had noticed them walking on board and alerted those inside. They had revealed themselves by their shoes. Over one hundred men were arrested. Our friend had slipped out. He now lives in Seattle, a political asylee. Those who stayed, some of them, were roped into the state's network of informers, like the Islamists and dealers. Snitchers, someone had called them in the months after as the trial progressed and we sat at cafés like this one, hesitantly, talking about their fate. Survivors, another had said.

The transaction of words across the table was clear. Dido burst forward. His plastic chair pushed onto its hind legs and then over onto the floor. I watched as he took fierce strides towards them. His legs were skinny, his jeans sat just below the line of his boxers. He had lost weight over the past year, his face now drawn. He had stopped wearing a tie some time ago and only ever wore plain T-shirts and colored hoodies. Even in the summer. He would tell me to meet him at *El Borsa*, and I could spot him by his hood, which was always over his head. We didn't speak about all that much anymore, not the way we used to, even though we spent hours at cafés on the pedestrian streets in downtown together. His eyes still twinkled and his mouth was always verging on a smile, but he had become somewhat dispirited. One afternoon I noticed his engagement ring was off. I asked. He shrugged. It's over. His second fiancée. She isn't right anymore. Why? Don't want to talk about it. I said nothing but could see he was hurt, so tried to change subject, make conversation. I brought up my book again. The main narrator, what did he think, how should I deal with *form*? We were both interested in this, what a new Egyptian modernism, founded in the vernacular, might be, and some afternoons Dido would spontaneously want to talk about it, things I should read around it, an idea he had, even as he concurrently wanted me to put my writing aside and join the movement. But that afternoon he swung back onto the hind legs of his chair, pulled the cords of his hoodie, tucked his head deeper in. We sat in silence. His friends, overlapping groups of old leftists and a new, much younger generation of activists, all looked much like him. Less in their dress, but more so in their demeanor. Dido's red hood slipped off his head as he barged toward the young men. He lowered his face between them, clenched his fists. I made out the insults. Heads had turned. The café paused. The yellow-headbanded boy put his hands up as if in surrender, or appeal. Dido flicked his hand in the air and swore. He paused over them. It might have been less than a minute that felt like time had stopped. *Traitors*, he said under his breath as he strode back towards me and sat with a thud. He became incensed when I expressed a sympathy, suggesting that they were only trying to find a way of making a life for themselves, that he should be more forgiving.

It wasn't that many weeks later that Uncle had died, and at the funeral Dido ignored me. He walked into the mosque, kissed Mama, Aunty, Taunte, wiping both his and also her tears, then sauntered to the farthest row of chairs and sat down, burying his head in his phone. I couldn't remember ever having seen him cry before. The mosque had been packed. People poured in. Uncle seemed to have known everyone. Yousra was there, the widow of Sadat was there, for a moment even the pop star Amr Diab. The farmers came from Faiyûm. The service was held in the only mosque in the city that allowed men and women to be seated in the same large hall. I imagined that Dido might not have come had we been segregated. I watched him, kept my eye on him, but hadn't noticed when he left. Mama remarked later how withdrawn he seemed. A cousin asked why we weren't speaking, then said she worried that his activism had become as much about intolerance to experiences that strayed from his ideals as it was the tolerance he preached. She worried he was too influenced by those around him. I imagined Uncle would have said he was hardened by life. It saddened me, the sudden change in him, our distance, but I wondered if perhaps he was also simply brokenhearted.

Everything seemed to happen that summer. It was the end of August. I had come up the stairs with a bag of oranges for Mama and found the door open. I peered into the living room. She was sat on the sofa, TV on, muted. A talk show was playing. It seemed to be a program about Ahmed Zeweil. Mama had got rid of Granny's fan some summers before, but the new plastic one seemed to have become equally as noisy. It drowned out my footsteps. I walked in. Mama's face was to the television, but I could feel her neck, her entire being, turn towards me. She spoke without moving, her eyes focused on an abstract point on the screen. I could feel the words wrestle with her throat, until eventually they came out. Drawn, slow, deliberate. I have some news, she said. She started by telling me about a dream she had the week before, in which Baba had tapped her on the shoulder. I stood, didn't say anything, waited. She spoke.

Apparently.

Your Baba is back.

He is staying at your aunts'.

He would like to see you.

As you can imagine, he has been through a rough time.

I stared at Mama, then the TV. I stood in silence for a moment. She sat in silence for a moment. My body felt transfixed. My mind blank before it began to spin. I wanted to ask where he had come back from, how long he was staying. Had she spoken to him, had he come to the house? *What kind of rough time?* Mama pressed the mute button to bring back the sound. I stood there for as long as I could in my daze, staring at her steely profile, then I turned around and moved, as if automated, in the direction of the kitchen. I emptied the bag of oranges into the white plastic basin in the sink. Turned the tap on. Took the blue Bril liquid soap and squirted some into the container. I held the tap until the soap had foamed over the oranges. Turned it off. Stared at nothing in particular for a long time. I went onto the balcony and looked out at our neighbor's building, and all the apartments I had watched for years with their shutters closed. Baba was back. Had anyone seen him? Would they know who he was? My lip trembled, and I bit on it. Hours might have passed. Baba was back. I tried to mentally conjure who an older Baba might be. Would his hair have grayed, thinned, run the span of its life course, leaving him bald? Would the years have eroded his frame, making him smaller? Would he still walk as he used to, his head held high as if pushed up at the chin by a father's disapproving thumb, his steps slow, deliberate, his shoulders tilted back? Would he laugh in the way I remembered, throwing his whole head, his neck, his chest, back in a forceful bellow? Everyone had always remarked on Baba's laugh, how emphatic it was. I remembered what Uncle said about memories. All my own overwritten memories were ones I wished to have back. I imagined the memory of Baba was one Uncle would have chosen to preserve. For a moment, standing on the balcony, seeking balance in Mama's words, I wondered if it might have been what I would wish I could choose too.

In those first weeks I couldn't look at Baba for long without needing to turn away. We would meet every few days and sit by the pool at the club in a near silence, watching people walk by. I hadn't anticipated the lapse of time would hang so heavy on his face, or maybe I simply hadn't known what to expect. Baba's lip trembled, and I would feel him staring at me, taking me in, assessing the change, the years, who I had become. I thought Dido had probably been right,.I felt an anger, but didn't know what to do with it, what to make of it, even where it belonged. I started to get irritated by most everything Baba said. We bickered, argued, I felt resentment, both at his absence and now his presence. Things felt fraught, and at moments I even wished he wasn't there.

Months later I called Baba spontaneously, exhilarated after the first day of protests, wanting to share my excitement. There was no cell reception those days, the government had shut it off, and Baba began to call early every morning on the landline, just after dawn, and then again late at night, past two a.m., when he knew I came home. Our relationship found a grounding in politics, and then towards the end of that first year, when Baba came to terms with the reality that he couldn't slip back into the life he had left behind, he talked about finding himself a wife. He would speak to me about the cycles of history, how we were reliving a past, almost as if déjà vu, then he would trail off about companionship. Baba was lonely. He was also deeply skeptical. He repeated himself, a little like Grandmama used to, telling me about his generation, their experience, the losses and disappointments of his youth. We have lived it all before, he said, we already tried it. He didn't want my hopes to be too high.

At first I thought it was just the emotional lesions of life, Baba's weariness. He seemed to have become a pessimist, not the Baba I had remembered or imagined him to be. I kept a journal every day of that first year he was back. I wrote down everything he said, everything I remembered of our conversations, our days, his expressions, what he was wearing, what he would order to eat. I wrote down how I felt, the vacillating emotions, the realizations, the chasms between

the memories and stories I had imagined, pieced together, held close, and the truth of who Baba was, who
he had become. Now I pick up the notebook chronicling that time, starting in the summer of 2010. On
every page I take note of the question marks. The
word *truth* seems to repeat itself multiple times on
each page. My handwriting is barely legible.

I became less and less reactionary to Baba's pessimism
when I fully digested all that he had been through.
Then day by day, as the months drew on, I saw intima-
tions of change. His group of friends got larger. Those
who had once pursued him through government and
legal cases now sat side by side, also victims of this
cyclical history I was just beginning to grasp in the
aftermath of uprising. They would sit around rusted
tables pulled together, piles of newspapers between
them, peanuts in brown bags, sometimes sandwiches
of *foul* and *taamiya*, debating the news. The army will
do this. The Islamists will do that. My source tells me
the Americans forced the army to let Morsi win. It
was forged. I have documents proving it. Impossible. I
swear. They all had theories, sources, certainty. Once
an outer mourning had left and marked their faces,
they all began to laugh, about the old days, how they

used to live. One man: Remember when I was a Basha. He would then throw his head back and growl with laughter. Another: At this time one year ago I would be sitting down to drink tea with Mubarak and briefing him. And look at me now, practically in my boxers, being served stale bread. Roaring laughter. Baba pointed to one man one morning. He looks at least ninety, doesn't he? I nodded. But you will never believe that he is actually my age. We did business together. He ran the most successful cement business. He supplied me the raw materials for the factory. They put him in jail. They couldn't benefit in any way because he was so straight. They forged papers. Ten years, look at what they did to him. There was a time when either you stayed and lost your life, or you fled. Baba pushed his glasses up his nose. He pointed to another man. Then a woman. Then a couple in the distance. Those two, he would begin, and then tell me their story. Here is the former state security agent. This used to be the most successful currency trader. This man used to be the minister of foreign affairs. This man was Mubarak's adviser on Israel. This man was his photographer. This good-looking man is the son of the most glamorous couple in show business. This woman used to be Miss Egypt. Once the most important newspaper columnist in the Arab world. This man used to own a bank until they nationalized and confiscated it. He lost everything. If you had heard this woman's voice when she was young . . . Age hasn't been so kind to this lady here.

I begin most days at the club with Baba now, surrounded by his friends of circumstance. I run while he swims, and then we have coffee before I go home to work. We have never really spoken about his years of absence. I have a vague idea of what happened, the problems, his refusal to offer a major contract he had tendered to one of the president's sons, the corruption charges they manufactured and landed him with, case after case, unrelentingly. Where he went, what his life was like during those years, I have pieced together stories, but never ask questions, never raise the conversation, despite still holding it all close. Sometimes Baba will make mention of what life has taught him. After all I have been through, he will say. I nod, then try to change the subject, to steer conversation to something else. I came to understand from my own experience that Baba had been a victim too. They had broken him. I knew he would also never really come to terms with being absent when Grandmama had died. I could see all this in his face, every single day, the nervous tic that marked him. The corner of his right lip would turn downward for a second, pulling his whole face into a droop, before turning up again. He would then scrunch his nose, as if in discomfort, and blink. It was the kind of blink that lasted longer than necessary. The kind of blink you took notice of. It was almost as if he were trying to blink something out of his eye, or perhaps even his memory.

Although Baba's twitch seems to have lessened these days, I now understand what Dido used to say about my anger, that Baba's circumstances should have unleashed it. Only in writing this now, reflecting back on it all, projecting myself into these pasts, real and imagined, considering the last few years, do I understand that in the end it did. Things built up; our frustrations, desires. And we all released something, given the chance. Our breaking point was about opportunity, human emotion being offered an outlet, in tandem discovering its source. In a notebook I write this down. I also make note of my anger. I seem to have developed more empathy than anger. *Is this normal,* I write. I find that note now, circled in a green pen and underlined twice. It is dated December 31, 2012. My desire to pull Baba from a past that lurked at every corner and bring him into a new present felt extreme during that time. I wanted him to be excited about revolution, to shake off his skepticism, the shadow of past lives. I wondered, constantly, about memories overwritten, what it would take to overwrite his— all he had seen, those years of hiding and distance. I now realize that it takes either a larger trauma or fleeting euphoria to erase what was. I can't imagine what might efface our most recent disappointments, except maybe the passing incandescence of love.

I ask the taxi to pull over just after the Azhar Mosque. A year ago to this day in July, the city was at a standstill. Millions in the streets calling for the ouster of then-president Morsi. I counted myself among them. Most friends, acquaintances, colleagues I know, even those who now say his ouster was a coup, were there with me. Baba found the crowds too much and preferred to watch it all on television, calling me every hour or so for an update from the ground. Mama had come with me. She had started to attend more protests than I. She had been scared when the protests first started those years ago, but then after a few, she said she felt liberated. She would take her flag and march, chant, clap, wave her arms emphatically with the crowds. I didn't know it then, but her stamina came to outlast mine. I hear her voice in my head now as I step onto the street. A building-size flyer of the new president, Sisi, hangs off the sides of one, two, I count five buildings on the street. Time changes perspectives, she used to say. Things become darker, like paint. I also think of Uncle, warning Dido and me that in life we have to assess things and always take a position. It's all relative, he told us. I wonder if my position is too often ambiguous. A position of trying to weigh things and assess and be objective is sometimes a clear position, and sometimes no position at all. I think a lot about what it means to be a witness, the responsibility of it. I wonder about my writing, if fiction is a political statement or simply no position. Is the silence of objectivity and being an observer, *witness*, the same as complicity? This question occupies me. H categorically tells me it is not. She says I shouldn't mix things. She no longer believes that everything in the universe is connected, but she says that intent is the most important thing. What is one's intention? I imagine it's the position of the yogi, which she now is, teaching classes every day. I know that Dido thinks otherwise, and it makes me question why am I more forbearing in the name of change when he only stands by the absolute. These thoughts stay with me as I give the taxi two pounds more than the tolled fare. When the meter was first introduced, we all complained and said it was thievery. Then we forgot. Swiftly. I appreciate a meter after a lifetime of bargaining. Nothing was ever enough, no matter what you gave.

I maneuver myself through the cars that are paused at an angle, waiting midstreet for takers. It's midday in the summer heat, and tourists are scarce. Travel warnings are reissued for Egypt each month. I spot a couple coming out of the mosque with backpacks, she with a scarf draped lightly over her head. I walk towards the pavement. The call to prayer filters in somewhere from a distance, echoing, one muezzin mimicking the next. No matter what time of day it is, there always seems to be the chant of prayer. An old man, frail, in a paper-thin white shirt, leaning over a cane, shuffles in my direction. I dip into my pocket and pull at the corner of a five-pound note. I scrunch it into my hand. I watch the man as he moves towards me. He doesn't look up, and people clear the way, moving from his path. Most pedestrians are this way, they walk, they cross, they move in the direction they are going without looking up, or to either side. He walks right by me, not raising his head. I turn around, watch him, then step forward towards the alley. It is lined with cavities, stalls, layered with brightly colored T-shirts, socks, bras, underwear, galabias, scarves, ties. Some of the things are made locally, but most of them, more and more, are from

China, shipped across the world to accumulate in homes as junk. SpongeBob T-shirts. PedEggs. Wind-up dolls. Padding the walls of one stall are mattresses, lined, piled, straight, at an angle. Two boys lie around playing Nintendo. In another, mesh sacks overflow with Egyptian cotton. This was the founding street of Cairo. It's hard to stop, to browse. What remains of its width fits two people and the bustle is intense. To pause means to obstruct the entire one-kilometer stretch, from one side of the Old City to the other. Music filters out of a crackling radio somewhere, Quran plays like a drone in the background. When I look up, I see the glistening silver dome of the Citadel perched on a limestone rock above the old city. I pause and then sidestep into a shop. *Makhazin Sono Cairo,* I say. The man gets up from his stool. Sticks his head of out of his stall. Points to a line of neon plastic beach balls hanging from one shop. Gives me directions. I thank him, bowing my head. He asks if I will stay and have a glass of tea. I thank him again. Something cold to drink? Thank you. You don't like our tea? It's not that. Give us the opportunity to host you. Thank you, but I have to meet someone. He laughs. In a breathing space between people I step back into the moving crowd. I mimic the steps of the women before me. In her I find my pace.

The storeroom of Sono Cairo is a shuttered garage space on an offshoot of the once-street-now-alley. A young man sits on the pavement. A cigarette is perched behind his ear. He seems to know who I am. Mohamed, he says. Hag Ahmed told me to be at your service. I nod my head. Thank him. He gets up, pulls at the waist of his sagging jeans. Turns. With all his force, he pushes up the corrugated metal shutter gate. Dust blows onto both of us. We turn our heads. I shield my eyes with my arm. Sorry. You're the first person to come here in years, he says. No worries at all, I say. I dust myself. We step forward into the dark. A single lightbulb hangs from a bare wire. A flyer has been pushed in the space between the floor and the shutter. I bend and pick it up. He looks. His laugh is like a smirk. I can't tell if it's one of ridicule or disillusionment. The flyer is denouncing Morsi's ouster, calling for solidarity with the democratically elected government and *legitimate* president. I take Mohamed in, with his scraggly beard, and wonder what his views might be. I say nothing and begin sifting through boxes, piles, stacks, of old vinyl. Dust coats everything. Mohamed hovers nearby. I feel him. He shifts from one foot to the other. Watches me. I keep my head down, leafing through records. Our silence seems to be on pause. He volunteers. *By the way, I am not a Brother, but I supported Morsi. All this area we supported Morsi. They used to do good for us, the Brothers. They helped as a lot. Financially, I mean. But we were going down a bad path.* I have become weary about engaging in political conversation. Hopefully good will come, I say. I turn my head down and continue flipping through the stacks. He stands over me for a minute, then moves to the other side of the room. *Just so you know, the Brothers would have destroyed this storeroom and all these records had they stayed in power. Music is a sin for them, you know. Where in the Quran does it say music is a sin? For them it was a sin. They were going to teach us about our own religion?* He walks back to me holding a record. With the sleeve of his shirt he dusts it. He reads. It's one of Umm Kulthum's rarest. They printed only 850 copies that were quickly taken off the market. Someone criticized her voice. They compared it to a young and upcoming male singer. Mohamed tells me she's his favorite singer of all time, and also his idol. I wonder if he knows she loved women. I know of the record in his hands but have never heard it. It's a collector's item, sold for hundreds of dollars online. He tells me I can have it for one hundred pounds. I tilt my head and consider bargaining, then put it in my pile. We talk about music and what I'm looking for. I pick up an old gramophone record of Asmahan. This, I tell him. He laughs. You know your music well. That's a rare one. He is surprised that someone of his generation would want vinyl. I shrug. He tells me the revolution has connected us to a past that preceded us. I nod, tell him I've gone back into our history books to understand. I've read everything. I can't believe all this I didn't know. You might not believe me, he says, but I have too. He's learning that history is repeating itself. We talk about Nasser. The first revolution. 1919. The Wafd revolting against the British. It wasn't really a revolution, he says. It was a popular uprising. I raise my eyebrows. But it was a revolt, I say. But there wasn't a change of a system. The country didn't completely change. The British didn't leave until years later. So what is a revolution? I ask. *1952.* But it was also a coup? He shakes his head. It can *only* be called a revolution. Could it have been both? People didn't take to the streets, it was just one system of power ousting, usurping, another. That's a coup? Yes, he says, but it was against something that didn't represent the people, so it was a revolution, for the people. Then 2011 was the same? I ask. That was a different kind of revolution, he says. There are different forms of revolution. But in the end all that happened is the army forced Mubarak to step down, as in '52? The people forced him out, he says. But the army also wanted that? They didn't want Gamal to succeed his father. They might have scripted this whole thing, *January 25*. He pauses. I offer: And 2013 was no different, really, except that millions and millions more came out.

We talk about 2011.

2013.

Does it matter if the people's movement calling for Morsi's ouster was quickly propped up by the state? In the end it was the people's desire, a sincere expression of what they wanted. He tilts his head and thinks for a long time. He isn't sure. It's something he feels conflicted about. I look into his eyes. I nod. I understand, I say. He shares with me his life story. Hours pass. I leave the store with fifty records. We agree I'll come back next month. I tip him. He refuses. I insist. He accepts. He tells me the storeroom is mine.

I catch a taxi back in the direction of home. I ask if we can make a stop at the Anglo American Hospital. I'll slip in for just a few minutes, and then we'll continue. It will take me a minute, you can keep the meter running. He tells me he is at my service. Leans over, turns the meter on. It jumps to five pounds. The starting price is meant to be two and a half. I say nothing, make a mental note to keep my eye on it. Taxi drivers speed their meters up, the rest of us slow things down—the electricity meter, the gas meter. It's the only way to trump the government's stealing. It costs fifty pounds to slow your meter to save five hundred. We drive past the Azhar Mosque and curve around, up past Azhar Park, which was once a garbage dump, the largest in the city. To turn it into a park, they emptied eighty thousand truckloads of garbage. I ask the driver if he knew that. He brings his children here every month, he says. But they go the back way, from the door that costs twenty-five piastres entry, not the one on the main street. That one is for the rich, he says. The ticket is for a pound. Are you married? he asks I am not. How old are you? I lie. Why are you not married? I mutter about circumstances. He peers up to his mirror and makes eye contact. I look away, and he turns on the radio. Someone is talking about bilateral relations with Ethiopia and the historic feat of the new government in reaching a deal on the new dam. It marks a groundbreaking era. Egypt and Ethiopia are one, the man says. God save Sisi.

We drive through downtown. It has finally become easier to navigate the nucleus of the city. The big blocks that barricaded streets, dividing the police from the people, have come down. Road obstructions have been cleared. The square is open again. We pass Mohamed Mahmoud Street, and immediately I think

of betrayal. Not the betrayal of my father's generation, the one of defeat, but rather the betrayal of the
Brotherhood and police colluding in clashes one November three years ago. Dozens were killed. A friend
was raped in the process. Another had both arms
broken. At the morgue piles of young men had phone
numbers scrawled on their arms. When I asked, someone told me they were the numbers for home, their
mothers' numbers. They had left their houses knowing they might not return. Dido and I weren't talking
at the time, and I scanned that morgue, terrified he
might be there too, piled among the rest. My memories of crossing that street, of university, of my paraly-
sis in the face of the city, have been overwritten. Then
overwritten again. The scars of our most recent history are everywhere. I have to dig, consciously project
myself back into an imagined past as I sit here now,
writing, to recall going there with Baba. It was on the
same street corner where Baba saw the Israeli jets that
I first saw the square full, first experienced tear gas,
saw my first dead body, shot from behind. I think
of Uncle constantly and the conversations we had. I
imagine that if he were still alive and I told him now
that I wish I could preserve the older memories, erase
what they have been replaced by, he would tell me that
to be a witness to history is a burden for the chosen.

Others live day by day with no glimpse of anything remarkable, he would say, not even the pink sunsets when they come and color the city in its entirety, because how can you take pleasure in the sunset when it marks the end of your day and the total sum of tips you have earned, which is likely hardly enough. I imagine he would tell me what he had many times before, that what I have lived is an extraordinary gift, not something to be squandered. Some days I still just want to erase it all, shake off the shadow of disappointment. *The second defeat, our second Naksa.* I write this in a notebook and circle it many times.

The taxi turns and crosses onto the bridge with the lions. A year ago I never knew what to expect when I crossed that line at the end of the bridge towards the square. We anticipated, always, that something might erupt. Clashes. We checked the news before we went downtown. Before we went anywhere. Friends, family, checked on us by phone each hour. Remember? H asks me one day. I didn't.

We veer into the tree-lined side street where the Cairo Tower stands, famously built by Nasser, using CIA bribe money, to be the tallest structure in the city. At the hospital I walk towards the back garden and a barebones shed. The clinic looks better suited for a rural setting, much like the army shacks one sees crossing the Sinai desert, looking like abandoned relics from a past war. A woman at the front desk is eating a white cheese sandwich in *fino* bread. Another is on her phone. She is sharing a recipe for *kunafa*. The secret is taking it out of the oven ten minutes before it is ready. Then you add the syrup and let it cook for ten more. Exactly. Yes. Most add the syrup at the end. She shakes her head. I stand over them, waiting. I shift from one leg to the other. I look, trying to focus my stare, will them to turn to me. The sandwich is consumed. She wipes her mouth with toilet paper from a roll on her desk. Gathers the newspaper and crumbs. Scrunches them into a ball with one hand. Tilts her hips and with her buttocks pushes her chair back. Its legs screech against the tile floor. She pauses and takes a breath, then leans her wrists against her thighs and pushes herself up, still, to my surprise, chewing. Her eyeglasses slide to the tip of her nose. She walks towards a door in the corner of the room. Eventually I'm asked what I'm here for. Dr. Zaki. Do you have an appointment? I don't see your name here. He told you to come? What time did he tell you to come? You spoke to him personally. What's your name again? What time is your appointment? What number did you call him on? So you called him on his own number? Show me. Sit down.

I sit.

A Sudanese family of seven walks in. Their littlest boy comes straight up to me. Puts his hand on my thigh and climbs up onto my lap. He looks to be two. He puts his palms on my cheeks and smiles. The buzzer sounds, and I'm told to *go*. I lift and put him down. He holds on to my thigh. His mother tells him *off*. He follows me, then stops before the turn of the corner, where sight of his mother would be lost. I peer into Dr. Zaki's office. It is a cubicle large enough for two chairs and a desk. None of the doctors' offices in this outpatient annex have patient beds. Their walls are plastic. A cloud of smoke fills the room. I decipher his outline, pear-shaped, with rolls. I knock. He is sitting at a desk the width of a smart car. Piles of papers surround him. An ashtray rests precariously on the edge of his desk by his belly. A cigarette is in his mouth. Another, lit, is in the ashtray. He seems to alternate between the two. He notices me. *Come.* He says. *Sit.* I hold my breath and take a seat, trying not to inhale. I feel the smoke seep into my clothes, hair. A computer from 1986 is on his desk, swallowing most of it. I wonder if it works. He stands up. His belly rolls over and rests far below his waist. Two buttons have popped. He puts a cigarette in his mouth, scuffles sideways, peers into my face. I look at his feet.

He is in fabric bedroom slippers. He tries to exhale at an angle, but the smoke comes down between us. He gestures with his hand to push it away, then exhales again. He goes back to his desk, scribbles on a paper. Says. Take this cream twice a day. Come back in a month. What is it for, what is this from? Is it curable? Will it go away? I've been to many doctors already. How long will it take? He snaps that it will take time. He then sighs deeply. I apologize. Take the paper. Walk out backwards, pulling the door behind me.

The taxi driver connects two wires under his steering wheel and restarts the car with a jump. We drive around the curve of the island and past the club. I look into the fence, the hedge, at the construction. A billboard counts down the days. The army has taken a third more of the club and given it to *the youth*. We no longer, those of us who pay, have access to the horse track. Much of the golf course is gone, turned into football fields. The running track is being turned over to cyclists. The president is photographed every weekend cycling through the city. They print his photograph on the front page of the daily papers.

At home I listen to Fairuz. She sings of the winds of change on the coast, *Shat Iskandaria,* and of falling in love in the summer. In the kitchen I try to open the fridge door. It's old, and the rubber padding is like suction. It bursts open, and I'm thrust back. I take out an ice tray. Bang it on the sink counter. Take a hand-blown glass from the ledge by the stove. Put four cubes of ice into it. I make my ice with tap water but fill the glass with mineral water from a bottle. I take my pile of newspapers onto the terrace and sit on one of the old bamboo chairs that used to belong to Granny. My eyes drift through the mango trees. I think of the last time I was at that same hospital, two summers ago. A friend had called at ten p.m. I hadn't picked up. She texted. *It's urgent*. I called back. A mutual friend had been stabbed, multiple times, could I come? They found him in a pool of blood. Left for dead in his apartment. The paramedics say he had been there at least twenty-four hours. He had burn marks too, as if electrocuted. I had run out, grabbing just my keys, stopping a taxi, asking him to hurry. At the hospital I sprinted into the ER. There was commotion. I looked around. I saw familiar faces, but nobody registered as someone I knew. Our friend was on a stretcher. I leaned over him and peered. Stood in silence for a long time. I had looked at him, our friend, with his cloud-white face stained with clots of blood, his hair like clay, his body covered in sheets, motionless like a mummy, and wondered how he could survive, and even if he did, what kind of life he might have, if it would be worth it. We were in the hospital for hours and through the night until dawn as we waited, for news, a clue, a doctor who could tell us something, anything. They rolled him into a corridor and said the doctor was coming. An hour passed. Two. He was still in the corridor behind doors with signs warning about hygiene. A young man walked in, dressed in street clothes. He looked at our friend, pulled up his sheet, put it down again, and walked on. Eventually they rolled him out. We were still waiting for the doctor.

Plainclothes police and investigators and informers came and went, testimonies were taken. We waited and watched as people were rushed into the ER, as patients were rolled in and out of the operating room, as a young man came screaming, asking for a hospital bed, for help, for his mother, his dear only mother. *We have no beds,* a young nurse told him. *If you can find a free bed, you are very welcome to put your mother on it.* She then walked off, seemingly indifferent. Perhaps it was her mechanism for survival. I had stood and watched as the young man screamed and shouted and tugged at his own shirt in frustration and people gathered to try to calm him, and me,. I wondered if he had a gun. They seemed to be everywhere those days, that first year of revolution. In the background a woman was wailing for help, and others were asking for extra blankets, a chair, syringe, painkillers, a doctor. *We're out of supplies* was invariably the response, *if you find any you'll be lucky.* What were the chances of anyone surviving here, and even if they did, this—the chaos, the nonchalance—showed the value of a life in a country unable to accommodate or contain those it already hosts. *This has nothing to do with riots or revolution, but the very fundamentals of an overtaxed and corrupt bureaucracy and the cycles of circumstance and life. This is the type of bureaucracy so far gone that there is no one left to argue with, no one to turn to with grievances. It has been this way for years.* I wrote this down into a spiral notebook one night as dawn approached. Our friend survived. Six months later and after many surgeries and with the acceptance of disability. This was to be alive, to be a survivor. This was life, to have gotten lucky. Nine months later the killer was found. He had stabbed five people that night alone. Three of them dead. He had lost his mind after the revolution. So the police said. I remember his picture, the mug shot. A tender-looking boy, absent in his eyes. I play through all this, sifting. The music suddenly stops, cutting Fairuz midsentence. I get up and go inside.

The power is out again. It happens every few hours. People mutter about inconvenience and the government's inability to fix the problem, its incompetence, but real grievances are mild. I go back onto the balcony and sit down. I pick up the newspapers from the floor beside me and put them on my lap. I skim them, one by one, first page, third page, crime page. Most of the headlines seem the same. Most of the names are people I now know. Every day there is some mention of Dido and the other eleven activists in jail pending trial. Mama says it has been a crash course in life.

There is a new checkpoint near the house. I approach it and slow down. Two armed, masked members of the special forces stand by metal barricades. Two others in plain clothes stand with them. Usually they wave everyone by, barely looking into cars or at faces. They stop me. Ask for my licenses, my ID. I reach for my wallet. The officer looks. Turns them over. Shuffles them like a deck. Hands them back to me, looking at the next car. I look up at him. You can go. It's early for a checkpoint, but I see another at the foot of the bridge. Pass one at the end of a ramp. Each day in the newspapers there is a story of an officer shot, a drive-by checkpoint shooting. On Facebook I read that the stories are contrived. Fear-mongering to justify the crackdown on Islamists. Most people I know don't seem to have objections. People talk about relativity, and how we are better off than before.

I drive around the island, slowing as I approach the club. They ask me to open the trunk of my car. Check it halfheartedly. Wave me in. I park, walk through the gardens of flowers, past the golf course, through the parking lot, up the steps towards the pool. I see Baba at the other end, sitting alone. I kiss him on one cheek and sit down. What news? I ask. He tells me the weather is beautiful. I nod. How have you spent your morning? Why are you sitting alone? Where are your friends? He shrugs. He doesn't know why no one has shown up today. A young man in orange overalls comes with a tray. He smiles and salutes us. What can I bring you today? Baba asks for a large grapefruit juice with no ice. I ask for a coffee, full-cream milk. Did you see the story of Dido in the paper today? He did. I know that Baba sees some of his younger self in Dido. As a young boy Grandpapa would drop him off at university and gesture with his fingers over his mouth like a zip. *We don't want any talk of politics, son,* to which Baba would bow his head slightly and respond, *Yes sir.* He would get out of the car and talk of nothing but. He repeats to me the story. You were brave, I say. I simply had the gene of rebellion, he says. Most of his friends were conformists, but *he* had been arrested three times for protesting. His face lights up.

The revolution had brought Dido and me closer again, then as it began to create divides between all of us, it tore us even further apart. I had risen to the news of his arrest one day last winter, on charges of inciting anarchy, disrupting the state. There had been insinuations against him and his friends for months. They had already arrested, released, then rearrested some of them. It seemed a matter of time before they would come for him. One night outside the Israeli embassy I had watched him stand with others who were making Molotov cocktails and throwing them high into the sky toward its premises. I had been almost certain they would take him that night, even though his actions were just in words. During the initial months, I went to the jail to visit him alone. Our conversations were terse, uneasy. I talked to him about Baba, the news, the conspiracy theories circulating around everything. I told him a little about my own life, my writing, the short films I was dabbling with, ideas I had, my novel beginning to take shape. He would sit slightly hunched in his white prison outfit and listen. Prisoners had no choice but to meet the visitors who came for them, and he seemed to sit as if in obligation, answering me in monosyllables. In an earlier life I might have withdrawn, too conscious of myself to stay unwelcomed. I imagine it was the changes of the past few years that had made me bolder, more resilient, even as it fractured something else. Each week I would see the change in Dido's face, the stubble that eventually became a beard, his hair growing out, the very structure of his face transforming. I couldn't tell if it was just the thinning of his frame or if his bones were transmuting, responding to the sadness and the pressure. His face looked sharper, more grating. Eventually he began to warm to me. He started to ask questions. He told me that prison was breaking his soul and he was doing everything he could to fight that. They had deprived him of books and writing materials. They made sure he couldn't see the sky. He slept fourteen hours a day, curled into the corner of space he could claim in his cell meant for two, shared with eighteen. I could tell he felt guilty for what he perceived to be his weakness. One day he asked to see Baba. It had been almost thirty years.

. . .

It was the day of his birthday, early this summer. Baba insisted we stop and buy a cake. Or make it four cakes, he told the man serving us, whispering to me that Dido would have to share, we couldn't just go with one. We drove along the corniche to the outskirts of the city, past the suburbs of new developments, to the line of the horizon where the informal settlements begin. Baba approached the gate. I followed. He gave Dido's name. Showed his ID. Offered tip. We waited. Eventually Baba went back to the car and sat in the backseat, legs stretched out. I stood by the gate pacing. An hour passed until they let us in. We went through the maze of corridors and into a decrepit room. Dido was already waiting, sitting on a metal chair, a guard by his side.

It was hard to look at him, really look at him, that day, even though I saw him several times a month. In the gap between May and June, when they had stopped visiting privileges, he seemed to have aged. His voice had deepened, softened. Even his posture seemed changed. He had looked at me at one point, gestured to his face, and told me this is what happens when you wait each day without knowing what you are waiting for. In a way I understood. The aging onset by circumstance happens externally sometimes, but most often the process, the trauma, the real change, is of an inner kind. Dido understood as well as we did that his case was a political one. The charges were baseless. The three of us sat there that day and spoke in roundabout terms of sacrifice. Mama would have called it the luck of the draw. Uncle would have spoken about relativity and assessment. Baba, that day, called it opportunity. We were given twenty minutes, more than the ten I usually got. I imagined it was because Baba was there. We spent them mostly listening to him. He spoke about survival, the lessons he had learned. He mentioned Sonallah Ibrahim, who had found his purpose as a writer in jail. I was surprised to hear Baba quote from Khalil Gibran. At thirty minutes, the prison warden told Baba our time was up. Baba raised his hand as if to ask for pause, and without turning his head said, *Two more minutes.* The guard looked at him and said, *Ya Basha,* saluting him and walking off. Baba put his head down slowly and continued to talk. As we got up to leave, I could see tears accumulating at the bottom of his lids. Dido was also shaken. His face trembled unconcealed as he bit on his lip. Baba held his shoulder and pulled him forward. Hugged him tight. Patted his back. Patted it harder. I heard him whisper that he was proud of him, that he was much braver than he had ever been. On my shoulder Dido whispered to me that he was sorry, then without looking either of us in the eye, he turned around and made a small gesture of goodbye and disappeared through a door. The guard appeared to escort us out.

Mama says she can't visit Dido. It's too hard. The pictures in the newspaper are enough. They show him behind bars, in the courtroom cage, skeletal, unkempt. Instead she sends him notes with me, cooks his favorite foods, buys him gifts. I find her in the kitchen one morning painting eggs, coloring them in detail, like miniatures, filling a straw basket. Easter, she says. They missed it. Mama still works long hours doing translation jobs, but she has become involved with a community association, writes letters and petitions, joins marches, spends what free time she has walking around the city taking pictures of things that need to change: The garbage, broken pavements, stray dogs and cats. "Can anyone help this poor dog, it needs a home," she posted on Facebook one day not long ago. On another, "This garbage around our homes, we need to care more. Have we forgotten those eighteen days?" This summer she joined a campaign to save electricity and combat the power cuts. I came home one day to a flyer she had made slipped under my door. *Turn the lights off except in the room you are sitting in. Try to switch to power-saving bulbs. Unplug things. Don't leave your TV on standby.* The list went on. She distributed copies to every building on our street, then asked me to scan it to post to Facebook. Although I still see her weariness, I know something in her has shifted. She laughs more, for one. Sometimes when I visit Dido, I show him Mama's Facebook activism. He laughs and tells me he has been a good example. I nod and joke that maybe the genes are in the family after all.

Dido and I seem to have bridged our differences, the chasm that grew from the disparity of his means of fighting and mine. I think to myself that none of us really seem to be fighting anymore, but don't have the heart to tell Dido that few of his fellow activists, comrades, show up these days for the protests calling for his freedom. He has become a poster child but gets more attention internationally than he does here. I wonder if I told him that, what he would say. He doesn't seem to be as critical, as rigid, as he used to be. It might be age, or it might simply be prison tempering him, taking him closer to who he once was. He says it doesn't take an entire population to change the course of things and that we each have our calling. I realize how more and more he sounds like Uncle.

I still have Baba's university ID on my desk, propped against a pile of books. Although he hasn't been back to the house, he mentions it one day. I wonder how he knows, but don't ask. We are sitting by the pool. He tells me that he knew a revolution would change nothing. I write this into my phone, as I do much else he says. I spend most of my days alone at my desk trying to write. Much of that time seems to be spent not writing, thinking about writing, pacing as I think. I work until dark, and then as the city falls quiet. I stop when the distant echo of music fades. I know this means it is an hour before dawn.

I wake up early on the fourth Friday in August. Lying in bed, I try to conjure Granny and Nesma, to will them into presence. Some months ago Mama had said she felt Granny in her room. I remember years ago when she had said the same about Nesma, approaching the edge of her bed and sitting down. I wasn't sure if she meant it literally, or if it was about resolution, coming to peace with something, letting go. I think of this more these days, what is contained between walls. I get out of bed and go into the bathroom. My sink is old, with two faucets—hot and cold. I try to scoop water from each one to make it lukewarm. I rinse my face. Brush my teeth. A travel clock sits on my sink. I time two minutes. I dry my face as I walk to the kitchen. Fill the kettle with water from the tap. Push open the shutters and stand looking out onto the backstreet. Nobody is there, and the city feels still. Behind me I listen to the water simmer and boil.

Upstairs I find Mama sitting on the balcony with her laptop, one Dido had given her, typing intensely. She had started keeping an online journal the day after Sisi was sworn in. It was May. We spent the evening before in the sitting room watching TV. There are dozens of channels now, broadcasting 24/7. Montages have escalated into dramatics. If it weren't Sisi, it would be terror. They repeat this, reminding us of the past. *Don't forget, these people are the ones who murdered Sadat. Don't forget what they did to Nasser. Don't forget Luxor. Don't forget Kosheh. Don't forget. Don't forget. Don't forget. Don't forget. Don't forget.* Images of the Luxor massacre. Clips inciting violence. Terrorized Christians. Bearded men butchering, pushing youth off buildings, armed. Figures flash across screens. Killed by terrorists. Massacred. Persecuted. Dead. Images of Sisi. Most people I know voted for him. Mama, Baba, even H. What other choice did we have? If you had given me another option. Me, I had slept through that day, waking up only after the ballots had closed.

Baba called the house the day of his inauguration. He had taken to calling us with news. Switch on the TV, he would say, and we would, without asking why. The broadcast started in the late afternoon, hours of camera roll of an empty hall and desolate palace grounds, which we watched on mute. Eventually cameras focused on the many dignitaries arriving, but the sun had set before the ceremony began, a mercurial orange. I got up and went to the kitchen. Walked onto the oval balcony and looked out. It was one of those nights when the building opposite our house was dark, except for the windows, the little outlets of life, the flickering TV screens. I could hear nothing from anywhere except the occasional roar and wind of a passing car, generally at a distance. I stood and watched. Took note of the single apartment still shuttered, the neighbor who had lost her daughter. I hadn't seen her windows open since. The city seemed to be on pause. I watched and waited, until suddenly, from all directions, the air was filled with the outburst of ululations. From across the street in our neighbors' building, and from across the river and from the city all around. Fireworks, music, shrieks. I rushed back in. The new president swallowed the screen.

The next morning I found Mama in the kitchen wiping the counter. I had walked in with the newspapers and a glass of juice. It had become a habit, sitting on the balcony together before I went to the club to run and see Baba. I knew Mama had been thinking about the house from the comments she dropped over the years since the revolution. She spoke about a memory etched permanently inside her, about feeling reborn. One day mentioned the weight of a physical burden anchoring her down. That morning, as she sipped her coffee and we looked out onto the garden, I could feel her neck and shoulders slightly tense. It was always the sign she was going to address something uncomfortable. She looked out to the sliver of Nile or a point beyond or something in the garden or maybe just her mind's eye, and without turning her head, she paused before telling me she had something to say.

It has been three months since that moment, and in early August we began to pack. The conversations around leaving the house and what it might mean for how we live and all we have known have been few, and cautious. Mama turns seventy this year. She sleeps in the bedroom she was born in. I can't imagine what a new life might mean, even though in ways she already has one. Mostly we have sorted through things on our own, but we have looked through albums together, told stories, laughed. We found Baba's ring together, in the back of a drawer stuffed with his papers. Mama talks of a party, opening the house to all those who haven't been here in years. I want to invite everyone, she tells me. Sitting on the balcony I ask her, hesitantly, if Baba can come. It has been thirty years since he set foot in this house that once was his home. Mama looks at me, eyes wide. She puts her mug down. Her neck stiffens, then relaxes. I tell her I wish Uncle were alive. She dreams of him often, she says. I wonder what Nesma and Granny would think. She looks at me, and I hold her gaze. I watch as she then turns her neck, puts her hand onto the side of her chair, as if seeking support, and looks in the direction of the Nile.

ACKNOWLEDGMENTS

TK

TK